TRUST ME, I WON'T LEAVE!

Vaishali Hamlai is an Oman-based author who has published four books. Her fifth book, *Trust Me, I Won't Leave*, talks about toxic relationships and how they impact those stuck in it.

Drawing from recent societal norms, and sharing her unique take on them, she aims to make reading easy and relatable through her writing.

Vaishali holds a Master's degree in Human Resource Management. Being certified in Meyers-Brigg Type Indicator administration, she has a good hold on the complexities of the mind and soul that translate into human behaviour.

Raised in Mumbai, she wrote her first book, *Rhea@Suraksha*, drawing from her real-life experiences. Her second book, *Down Under*, deals with racism, while the third, *Mind Trap*, is a self-help book about ways to make the mind stronger. Her fourth book *Through the Open Window* depicts how love can create, destroy and recreate.

Hamlai also writes for a column called 'Beyond Words' in the newspaper *Muscat Daily*.

Reach her at:
Instagram: @hamlaivaishali
Twitter: @HamlaiWriter
Facebook: Vaishali Hamlai - Fiction Writer

Also by the author

Through the Open Window

TRUST ME, I WON'T LEAVE!

Vaishali Hamlai

RUPA

Published by
Rupa Publications India Pvt. Ltd 2022
7/16, Ansari Road, Daryaganj
New Delhi 110002

Sales centres:
Allahabad Bengaluru Chennai
Hyderabad Jaipur Kathmandu
Kolkata Mumbai

Copyright © Vaishali Hamlai 2022

This is a work of fiction. Names, characters, places and
incidents are either the product of the author's imagination or are
used fictitiously and any resemblance to any actual person, living or dead,
events or locales is entirely coincidental.

All rights reserved.
No part of this publication may be reproduced, transmitted,
or stored in a retrieval system, in any form or by any means,
electronic, mechanical, photocopying, recording or otherwise,
without the prior permission of the publisher.

P-ISBN: 978-93-5520-909-2
E-ISBN: 978-93-5520-910-8

First impression 2022

10 9 8 7 6 5 4 3 2 1

The moral right of the author has been asserted.

Printed in India

This book is sold subject to the condition that it shall not,
by way of trade or otherwise, be lent, resold, hired out, or otherwise
circulated, without the publisher's prior consent, in any form of
binding or cover other than that in which it is published.

Prelude

Once upon a time, there was a love story... There was a king and there was a queen. The king and queen died, and the story ended tragically.

But in my story, there is a difference. No one died, and that was the tragedy...

1

There are two sides to a coin and what we see is only a single side. We assume that there's another side, because it's obvious that there is. But what happens when the coin is unusual? One's confidence in reality or truth is as certain as the existence of the other side of the coin. This is a story of the side that is not seen, whose existence is never doubted.

I am the girl-next-door you see in the movies and television series. I am also not the girl-next-door you see in movies and television series. The adventurous girl who can skydive in a wink. The girl who cries at the end of the film where her love is doomed. I am everyone and no one. That is me.

Sitting on the balustrade of the balcony, my thoughts spread. Should I try to jump from the porch of the first floor? Do I need to learn to fly? The absurdity of the thought did not puzzle me. Either way, the thought seemed perfect…

The rental flat at my disposal bent towards a general inertia—there seemed to be days when the leaves forgot to rustle and the wind denied a visit. My neighbour, being particularly suspicious, always came right out when I felt particularly unhappy. Like he had intuited it and naturally walked out to spy on me. Either way, it worked in my favour. It kept me alive and unharmed. My landlady usually passed out after dinner and woke early, before dawn. She was 80 and lived alone. She held a special place in my heart.

No, I have never harmed myself out of sheer disappointment, but the thoughts have unquestionably existed and been predominant.

There was calmness in the air. Sometimes the calm crossed over into tranquillity, and then went beyond to enter a cryptic zone.

Away from the busy streets, this old ramshackle building was nestled way inside the lanes of the city. Sometimes it felt like not being a part of the city. Although right at the heart of it, businesses didn't conjure up in this corner of the street. Not many knew of the existence of such a street in the neighbourhood.

The trees virtually closed in at the turn of the street. It looked like a dead road on the horizon from the outside. My building was surrounded by Neem trees, making it impossible to see it with naked eyes. The nights were quiet, with owls peeping inside the house like they belonged there too, and the morning brought parrots, chirping songs of love.

Walking back into my one-bedroom apartment I see a neatly wrapped white muslin cloth. There is some Pomfret fish curry with a few Neer dosas. My landlady brought them for me. It remains untouched on the thick bamboo coaster of my modular kitchen countertop. I just couldn't bring myself to eat. Eating is an activity for those who lack energy, who are probably hungry. For me, since childhood, food has only been a source of fuel and nothing else. Cravings for food was alien to my digestive system. Perhaps because I associated food with need, which may or may not be fulfilled. My desperate need for independence made me want to be independent of any need.

My next-door neighbour, Abhi, was a young gentleman who had been very kind to me. One year ago, he was my saving grace.

I always thought that men were another species altogether. Men are born to fulfil a number of prophecies—particularly in our societies. We, women, are born for just one purpose: to serve men. I remember, when I was little I used to play with dolls; and while visiting grand-aunts they would bless me with a particular benediction: 'may you find a good husband.' Deep down, in their hearts, they too knew that good husbands don't come easy. You need divine intervention, abetted by cycles of fasting and prayers, to get one. We, the girls, were required to behave in a particular manner so that everyone in the locality knew us to be docile, sociable and worthy of marriage. So, we were groomed to be subservient to a man's will once we grew up.

This might seem like ancestors haunting the current generation. Our elders will tell us that this is all history—we are no longer *that* traditional, women are now treated as equal to men in all ways. But alas, we still have a long way to go.

Pale moonlight spilled over the building and glinted off

the windows. A few stars peeped out of the grey heavy clouds and tried to shine. The inmates of the building seemed like they were in the grasp of a silent, depthless sleep for the entire area was airless and tight. The night-time wind was blowing, carrying with it a familiar smell—that of stale garbage from the dump.

I never felt lonely as I found freedom in my loneliness. Days and nights rolled into one another, melting away, interweaving and burying into each other. Time didn't seem to affect the house much. Days passed with an unseen regimen of light and shadow, probably observed only by the trees in our compound. And the withered, decayed leaves and the fast-spreading sadness made my apartment look like a lonely twinkling star in the dark sky. The windows, with their little mirrors positioned strategically to reflect the sun at different times of the day, added a shine to the otherwise drab exterior of the building.

My apartment responded only to the winds. The murky light filtered through the vertical louvres of the blinds, sometimes opening because of a gusty wind, singing a hauntingly distorted, repetitive tune. But my nights were alive. The nights spoke to the house. The nights played dark games, secret ones that only they knew. They embraced and loved the house in its dark corners, lurking shadows and whispering silence. The moonlight, when it visited the lonely house in triumph, rolled on the rough cobbled surface of the veranda and peeped playfully through the skylights to gaze at the hanging lamps in this sprawling one-bedroom apartment of mine. The money plants danced in the wind that crept in—a soft dance synchronized with the tinkling of the dangling crystal pieces, like the anklets on a dancer's feet.

I had come home late that night; the clock must have struck twelve just then. I was almost like Cinderella, but without her shoes. But this Cinderella had a faint stain of blood trickling from her lip.

At times, Abhi, my saviour, was found smoking a joint in the balcony (though he normally smoked indoors). Everyone knew this wasn't allowed, but the old landlady was fast asleep after having popped her sleeping pills. He knew her routine.

When he saw me, he didn't seem shocked or concerned, like anyone else would have been in this situation. He just held my hand and took me into his room and treated my split lip with care. There wasn't any sign of judgment or concern on his face. No creases on his forehead indicating surprise or shock; he was entirely emotionless. He was like a nurse treating a patient in an emergency ward. I, on the other hand, don't exactly remember much about that night. There was more alcohol in my stomach than food.

I noticed his shadow. He was following me upstairs to my apartment after I was bandaged up. It bothered me, but I felt brave and fearless. Probably because of my inebriated state. At first, it was a challenge to open the locks. I fumbled to get to the keys and finally managed to open the door.

Closing the door right on his face was certainly impudent of me. The kind of impudence shown by someone who is drugged or drunk, or is able to do what their mind wants. Ironically, I believe it should be a natural human state, but we like to mask ourselves up.

I remember, seeing through the French windows of my living room, the solitary shadow of the man walking back to his flat. There was surely something in his gait for it never left me, not for years to come. I also remember the damp odour in the air and the moonshine that bathed the buildings that night.

No single interaction with the mysterious neighbour after that. What happened earlier felt like an illusion. Maybe, there were other interactions that night I wanted to erase from my memory.

This memory was blurry…the night, the injury and the alcohol. It didn't allow a storyline. It had been an intense night with many questionable occurrences—to sum it up in a few words. But the youngish man with deep grey eyes stayed on my mind for quite some time.

I squinted at the sudden light that fell on my balcony.

The sun shone mightily right in the morning. I went to the balcony and stood there for a while, and then I got ready to go to the beach.

It wasn't the most comforting sight outside, but there was solace on the empty streets. Sometimes, it seemed like the road was automatically closed to those who didn't live there, like the streets disappeared into thin air. The sun baked the air bone-dry. The still air made everything in it breathless. The city looked ugly to me. The treeless, drab city appeared soulless for a moment. The air felt heavy on my cheeks as I drove through the mindless streets near the beach.

Sunday afternoons were a drag, so I ritually drove to the nearby beach. It was a rather sealed beach, with a small entry at the rear end. The area was rocky and unfortunately, people had turned it into a dumping yard for garbage. No one liked coming through that entrance, even though they knew that it allowed access to an isolated part of the beach. They couldn't deal with the stench. I took advantage of the situation, and made it my Sunday hide-out.

It was plain sailing for me. After all, I had been brought up in similar conditions. Not in *filth*, but symbolically speaking. I was raised in a toxic neighbourhood. I still remember the day I saved enough money to obtain a second-hand four-wheeler. They recommend that one should not squeeze the best deal from the needy, but I did so, to obtain this car. I was needy too; I recall telling myself. This car was needed by my alter ego. Sometimes, I feel like every person has two different persons within them—a self that is united with one's being, most of the times, and an alter self that is greedy and wants more. The car is a statement for most, but for me it was a need formed out of no need at all.

Once, I was walking through the train platform. It was a little later than 11.30 p.m. and I saw a man, with his dick sticking out of his torn pants. He was looking at me. This sight scared me for days and I decided to save enough to buy a second-hand car. Later, I realized that owning a car doesn't stop random strangers from masturbating or flashing at you. This city is sick: lesson learned and message received!

Driving around while listening to the radio, however, was my favourite routine to unwind. There were fewer human interactions—other than those I have already mentioned—during the weekends. I had no one to talk to, but I had no complaints. It was a welcome relief from having to indulge in small talk. Two days of sheer silence was food for my soul.

There were times when my thoughts would bring out the worst in me, but mostly it was a pretty sight on the beach. To walk on my bare feet and then to bury them inside the sand felt therapeutic.

That day, my cellphone was tucked into the side pocket of my beige chinos. My hands were cold and sweaty. Humidity made my hands sweat, and at times, people didn't want to shake hands with me because they remembered the horrors of their past handshake. I saw disgust flashing on their faces after they shook hands. Not that I cared for a handshake. My go-to greeting was always a folded hand; part of it was because I was aware of my own sweaty hands. But I think winter brought out the best in people. They were naturally kinder. I believe the weather has a bearing on the mood of the people. I was aware of this as I have often been on the receiving end of such behaviour. But taking all precautions to avoid sweating helped.

Winter in this city had a peculiar trait. Sometimes the city was pummelled by unprecedented winter storms. The wind swept the sands to the side of the beach, growing ever faster and thicker, trying to catch up with something that it had missed out in the prevailing damp heat.

I loved the beach during this time of the year. I imagined that I could taste the storms in the sand, the battering winds of hopelessness and torment that met me from time to time.

In this city, being dark skinned didn't help me much. But I had a perfect figure, which made me seem like an object worthy of possession within a wide group of people. In school, I had been ridiculed for my huge breasts, which had grown much before other girls of my age. Girls would make brusque comments about my breasts. There were rumours floating around school that the reason behind my large breasts was because I let boys fondle them. I received unnecessary and unwanted attention. Somehow, I was an object of discussion wherever I went. In school, I felt embarrassed by people's opinions about me, but as I grew older, I learned to push gossip under the carpet. I let it slide to a forbidden part of my brain, which now wasn't accessible—not even to me. The human mind is smart; it hides its pain and sends across stimuli to emphasize happiness. And we learn the balancing act in this unbalanced world.

Pain, for me, had become an illusionary mechanism that my mind could do away with by shutting down when it needed to. I practiced this and felt blameless.

I remember, one day, while walking back from school towards home, in the deadliest summer heat, I encountered an old man walking too close to me. He was following me. He was breathing heavily, right under my neck, murmuring four-lettered words. Unable to make out what was happening, I paced my walk faster than his own. I did not realize that I was sweating and walking very fast, so much so that I was breathless. I had left him behind, but the next day he was back, following me, breathing down my neck and murmuring. That man stalked me for almost a year. It was chilling to the marrow and I always felt terrorized. The days when he wasn't there, I would fear his shadow behind me. The thought of returning from school used to stress me out. I would fear anything behind me…be it a man, woman or even trees. But I kept my fear to myself. Never did it occur to me that I should tell an adult or that I should fight it out—scream when he tried to whisper in my ears and not be scared. I didn't know that I could report the matter and be safe. Now, when I am alone, there are nights when I dream of this man. I imagine that I fought him, fought him so hard that my hands hurt, but I fought back. I don't even remember the stalker's face clearly but the dent it left in my mind is enough to raise gooseflesh even today.

In the winter, when the fog rolled in and the cold winds whispered in an undertone, I once decided to take a walk after parking my car and the fear came back. The abandoned apartments, the rustle of the dry leaves resounding in the air. It left me with an eerie feeling.

In any case, time went by very slowly here. The memories of my childhood home had almost faded now. In my mind, a home always meant a small, packed space, spilling over with people and harmless squabbles. I had no home to match my childhood home now. This household belonged to the grown-up me and it was in order. Everything was routine. And my life was silent, except when I created some noise by switching on music or when I interacted with my neighbour (superficially, from a distance). Despite all this loneliness in my house, I was content in a way I hadn't ever known. Like someone who had been through a terrible storm and then found some breathing space.

But I realized that by remaining single I would be cruelly

conspicuous in a crowd of married couples in the locality. I only saw a few of them in the morning hours. They all remained forbiddingly distant in their bare tolerance of a single woman in their neighbourhood.

A child's fear is a world of its own. It has unknown corners; it has its skies and its abysses. It is a starless realm with deep and seemingly bottomless chasms into which no light can ever pierce a hole. Most psychological seeds are sown then, and grown over the years. These become the guiding forces and major influencers in our later years. What you hear and watch as a kid is what you mostly become. Only a few shine brighter in dingy surroundings.

I was different like that, I shone brighter and thrived more in crumpled situations.

2

Kneeling on my knees, my view was that of his hairy chest. It jolted me back to reality. Rather an ugly sight, but it satisfied my sexual cravings. Somehow, I didn't want to glance at the man pleasuring my body since he looked particularly distasteful while he was moaning.

I continuously repeated to myself. This was the last time I got myself into this predicament. Never again would I come to him for a booty call, or never would I accept one. But history repeats itself. And here I was—looking down his pants again. I blamed my eyesight. I felt that I was blind, and the hormones were all that were complicit in ushering me back into his dingy, small, disorderly apartment. It made me want to vomit when I looked around, but I didn't want to risk bringing him to my apartment. It would be disastrous to be caught by curious neighbours. Though the structure of the building was such that it made me think that no one else (other than the neighbour, landlady and myself) even lived there. Never did I see anyone walking in and out of the apartments. It was uninhabited, to say the least. I wondered whether the builders had considered the privacy of the inmates as their priority, or if this situation had just come to be. I believe that emotions can ruin businesses and hence, I have settled down with the solace that privacy was a mistake.

Even while having sex, my mind was attentive on his room, naming and numbering the items in the space. The ways and manners in which his room could be kept in order. How to make use of the extra space for room to walk. Even though I was no interior designer, I had a knack for keeping things in order. Things would not always look pretty and dainty, but I could vouch for being able to keep them in the least amount of space possible. Living in small-sized apartments had given me this superpower.

Some odd events had unfolded today. To start with: this escapade in the dead of afternoon at his place. I've come here in the past, late and after midnight.

Most nights, he would usually be on his balcony after midnight. It was my sign. But today, rather unusually and in the afternoon, when I was walking back to my apartment with a hunched shoulder, he grabbed me by the waist and swiftly swept me towards his door. I willingly walked into his room, feeling the urge to rip him apart. I wanted to make the most of his desires.

Attraction towards him was basic instinct. I was 34 and had my needs, so did he. It was a barter system and no one lost anything. Of course, my self-respect was at stake if anyone found out about it. Mostly though, it felt normal and natural. Maybe he felt the same way because he didn't mention it to anyone either. Either way, it was a neat deal.

Not that I was attracted to him; nor was he drawn to me. It worked best since we were not inclined to attachments. Today, he looked at me while kissing and raised his head, his scanty hair rushing at his hairline in a V-shape. He surely looked ugly. An ugly young man with crushed dreams. Not a flinch of hope gleamed through his eyes. I ridiculed him, even in my dismal state of arousal.

After some time, I felt heaven and nirvana. Strangely, those thin, lanky hands around me felt non-toxic and tougher, especially after I'd had multiple orgasms. But it wasn't just that.

I was dancing on his tunes in that moment of ecstasy. He was a drug that I needed. He now became my need.

I gathered my clothes while he ran to the toilet to hide his naked, corpulent, pudgy body; his stomach expanding from the sides and his butt being pulled due to gravity. It wasn't just his face that was ugly, but even his body was totally repulsive.

Now, it felt like I was getting along with that face. It didn't repulse me as much as before. This seemed like progress.

I slipped into my dress—the one I wore for the sheer convenience of being able to storm out as soon as possible. But today had been different. Firstly, we had sex in the afternoon. Secondly, I saw him from a closer distance compared to my blurry nightly visions of him. Then I stayed for coffee and cigarettes. As expected, it was a quiet affair, but both of us were present.

Around the house I saw many paintings of women of all shapes. None of the women in the paintings had a perfect body. None had the shape of a desirable woman. It made me cringe. It made me wonder if he liked having sex with me because I was not a conventionally perfect woman. I had the shape, but there were many things missing in me, which any normal man would otherwise desire.

He came out of the bathroom in his shorts and since it had already been decided that we would drink our afternoon coffee together, he swayed to his dilapidated but clean kitchen.

'Let me make you some coffee now.' He muttered to himself while moving towards the kitchen.

I didn't even bother to reciprocate with a 'thank you'.

He then pulled out some vessels to make coffee, then got some milk from the medium-sized silver refrigerator. I didn't rush into a conversation, though the urge to probe into the paintings was building inside me. But I am the queen of suppressing my urges. I can suppress any desire. It is another one of my superpowers.

We sat across the table and drank our coffee in silence. We didn't need to talk about anything, so we didn't. I was stealing sidelong glances at the paintings in between drags of my cigarette.

I finished off the coffee without looking at him even once. Neither did he.

Suddenly, I felt lonely. His unkempt house gave me a sense of his incompetence. But I enjoyed his pale, pimpled face and the traces of incapability and bad humour. He looked as tired as I felt. His hair was dishevelled and the dark circles beneath his blazing grey eyes made me feel sad.

After getting back to my apartment, I thought of him that evening and I wondered what he did for a living. He was always indoors. He never went to work. No one ever visited him. He seemed anti-social.

But it was none of my business. I had had my coffee and left that house. Never before had I thought of him and it worried me. Why was I thinking about him now? He kept popping into my head. He had made an impact on me that day. As I slept, I kept thinking of him. I did not feel a need to be with him…but maybe, someday, sometime, I would like to know him better.

It had been more than a hook-up, I realized.

That night, I fell asleep suddenly. The next day was going to be a challenge, plus I had a good workout in the afternoon. I woke up feeling like a zombie, without any particular dreams or even any memory of falling asleep. It felt as if I had put my head on the bed and had woken up within a second to the rising sun. I didn't know when I had fallen asleep, maybe around eleven o'clock, feeling exhausted while watching the documentary. Documentaries give me enough time to relax usually, but I woke up with the same exhaustion. But the thing about this kind of exhaustion is that it never feels like the morning has arrived. The exhaustion lasts till morning.

Actually, this exhaustion has been with me for some time now. Not days, not weeks, not months, maybe a year. The last time I felt alive was on New Year's Eve. I was drunk while hanging out with some acquaintances; no, I don't call anyone friends because I don't want to give them the opportunity to hurt me. In case they hurt me, I can always say that they weren't friends anyway. They were all acquaintances.

I always thought of love as unimportant. We tend to

attach too much importance to love between a man and a woman. It seemed like a muddle to me. I have always brushed thoughts of love aside, thinking of it as some sort of feeble concoction formed out of pity, care, contempt and common indifference. That's what we call love.

Moving back to the throbbing headache and the day ahead, I had to stand up and take a shower. After a double shot espresso, life was looking up. I dressed into a white salwar kameez and rushed out through the door. Reaching the office was an ordeal of its own. Mumbai's traffic had a character of its own. As it is, the weather remains damp and humid all year round. And to add to that, the monsoons were here. The sea, the overflowing lakes, the backwaters, the hills and mountains and the streets…are all bathed in this city. Nothing stops despite the rain, except for cars on the road. The cars wait and wait till you lose all the patience you can muster, till you burn out. And then, there are some days when the traffic moves like a breeze. Today was my day. Traffic was negligible. It made me check to see whether it was a public holiday or if a curfew had been called. But nothing like that had happened. I had to be in the office and continue the same mechanical actions, just like I have done over the past five years. Having done a doctorate on Mumbai's traffic, I had taken some short cuts, I realized.

I've lived here my whole life; the roads, back roads and short cuts are ingrained in my brain. It's only the people I don't understand. And Mumbai has its own share of diverse personalities who walk in and out; that's what makes it Mumbai.

I had driven from one multistory tower to another tower to the other tower. The whole place was full of towers and towers, but no place to go. Concrete beautiful towers that had everything to offer, except you weren't looking for anything particular.

I walked right past the long queue of people standing outside the elevators, into the orchid-covered sparkly lobby. The fluorescent lights and the reflective embossed Italian marble entrance gave the space an illusion that you were entering heaven—but it was like those jokes. Hell was recruiting and they had made the entrance appealing. My first day had been classic, I remember.

Today was not a lot different than the other days, but it would have its twist. Without thinking much, I knew I had to reach on time. So I took the steps. I was on the first floor. I didn't have to sweat like a pig compared to the others who had eleven floors to climb. I silently thanked god for being kind in some ways, if not most.

As I thumb-stamped the biometric like an illiterate person to enter my office, I had the misfortune of stepping into the sight of Deva—the loser of the century. If I was a loser of degree 10 he was a 100. He gave me a meek, unsure smile, which made me wonder if I too was somewhat like him. But then, I smiled back—a similar unsure twisting of lips—and stormed in.

Walking past the cafeteria was a curse in the morning. The stink of garlic and onions at such an unearthly hour made me sick. The clatter of the vessels and the chatter of the people perturbed me.

I sat on my slightly faded blue chair, put on my heavy headphones that could bury me in one day and sat down to take the first caller for the day.

To work at a call centre was a blessing since all you have to do is read from the script. You could be brain dead and still comply with the job specifications. Any change in question can be taken over by the ever-enthusiastic and extroverted leader who is in charge of the lines. I wanted to be the one who could answer all the questions, I had it in me. But no one believed in me.

Most of my battles with my callers had been lost, but I won them in my head. I always thanked my stars, glad to be an introvert so I could keep things to myself. At times, I did feel like screaming at the top of my voice and yell back 'GET LOST!' to them.

I was great at work, but I was the underdog. Though I hated the job, I respected it. It didn't give me a purpose, but it sure fed me well, enough to live a stress-free life. To be stress-free in Mumbai is an illusion, but maybe I lived that illusion. I did have stress but I knew I had created that myself. We'll get there soon enough.

Soon after answering my tenth caller, repeating the same response on how to fix his guitar strings and while talking about World War II, it was time for lunch. I was about to stand up from my seat when I blacked out. The last thing I remember was feeling a cramp in my stomach. I saw myself falling back on my seat.

After several minutes, or maybe just after a couple of minutes that felt like an hour, I heard faint voices.

'Meera!' Then a murmur. Then again, my name was called out. Louder and by someone else. 'Meera.'

'Meera, are you okay?'

Murmurs of 'call the emergency' brought me back to consciousness.

I sat up with a jolt and found that half of the call centre's employees were crowding near me. They were looking at me with bleak eyes and worried eyebrows. I'm sure some of them had learnt my name by now.

As soon as I woke up, Saira, whom I knew well, came with a glass of water.

'You scared me!' she said.

Saira had always been a worrier, and this must have shaken her up. I got up from my seat and tried to walk to a quieter area. Blackouts like these were a common phenomenon in my life, but for others it came as a shock. Saira looked at me as if she expected an explanation.

'It's nothing, don't worry,' I said quietly, glancing away from the stares. How I wished to be invisible. It's just not feasible to be visible to everyone all the time, the staring eyes and the pity is hard to ignore sometimes.

Quietly, I slid away with Saira, who had still not digested the incident. She looked at me like I was an alien. Finally, I had to speak.

'This is normal for me. Don't worry, I'm not dying.'

Then I realized I didn't know if it would bother her if I died. Not being able to decipher the answer just by looking at her expression, I asked after all.

'Would it bother you, if I die?' I candidly asked, wanting

to know the answer. Perhaps I sounded needy, but it's important to know if my being alive mattered to anyone. Clearly, it was an optimistic question to have asked. Saira looked away and blinked, as if she was trying to end the nightmare that unfolded before my eyes.

I had my answer!

But the optimist that I was, I believed that she hadn't replied since it was an odd question to ask. A normal person wouldn't ask such a question. But I wasn't anywhere close to normal. This was something I discovered when I was seven years old.

After lunch, I sat on my chair, wondering if anyone had even noticed that I was unconscious in this same spot a few hours ago. Some colleagues came up and asked how I felt after the blackout, but most of them stared at me like I was some leech trying to grab attention.

I overanalyse, at times...most times. The world around me needs to be analysed threadbare. I need a pastime and this was my favourite sport. To analyse, to mull over things and then, finally be happy with a conclusion.

I overheard a colleague talking in the lunch room. She is a mother, and she says, 'I tell my kids to just run around when they ask me what they should do.'

What! What was that? Why would a mother tell their kids to run around? Like rats, just run around, aimlessly? What good would come of that? Great parenting.

But who was I to question? It wasn't like I ever intended to have kids. I dread the thought! The process itself seems too long and cumbersome. You need a partner to impregnate yourself and then the usual duress. What put me off when I tried to think about having kids was the protrusion of the belly. Then, the thought of being pregnant—without the bulge—appeared absurd. I felt comfortable discarding the idea altogether.

Alongside my daily work at the call centre, I was also working on something different with my boss, Mr Rebello. He was a tiny, dingy smelling man. Sometimes, when I sat with him in his tiny cabin, it made me wonder—if he could be a manager, then I too could own this call centre.

Of course, the man knew about his own age, peeping through his receding hairline. He kept hiding it by pulling a few lone strands over his forehead, moving them from one side to the other. A lame attempt to mask his nudity. It was abhorrent, to say the least.

'Maybe a wig should be a good idea for you, Sir,' I said one day, unable to control my emotions.

Mr Rebello was livid and uneasy at my forthrightness. 'What are you talking about, Meera?'

He already knew about my eccentric behaviour but facing the barb wasn't easy for him.

The two of us were planning to open a new call centre in the city. Mr Rebello was a great manipulator and he had clearly walked up the career ladder through tactics of ass-licking and back-stabbing. He has been with the company ever since he joined as a trainee. The only person he was loyal to was himself. He was a poor manager and did not give anyone a chance to exhibit their talents as he feared revealing his poor leadership skills. And he probably forgave himself for all that he did to those who were like him. Or maybe, he never introspected. He was the type to never have any remorse. For him, everything was right and a part of the game—the rat race.

He understood my indifference to these things and never tried to rub me the wrong way. I was straightforward and meant business. At the office, I wore my attitude so well that my colleagues had either written me off as rude or granted me a non-existence status. I had no issues with this. I liked what I had turned myself into.

But for this project, Rebello didn't have a choice. He had to ask me for help because he was incapable of doing it all by himself.

Working alone on this project was not an option for him. He had to include me as I was the smartest, but also an irrelevant person in the company. No one would suspect the importance of the assignment if I was involved. He, the manipulator, had never any inhibition about setting such things in motion, but was definitely extremely cautious.

He was very circumspect in his statements and finally, he returned to my suggestion about his baldness. Which brings me back to the present.

'What you said...about my hair?' The boss made an inquiry.

He whispered, coming closer. It was pointless since the whole office had left. There were only some lone bachelors around since they hated their shared accommodations or detested their landlords.

'Is a wig a solution?' He glanced around if anyone was

snooping. 'I have also heard about hair transplants. I have gone to a hair specialist who recommended five sessions to start with. What do you think? Do you know anything about it?' He gave me a gummy smile.

Why would he care so much about what I think? I was no expert. I let the thought drift away in my head and I plainly nodded indifferently. Since I didn't speak much, he had learned to understand my body language. I wasn't mysterious. I just didn't have much to say. What could I have said? 'If you feel conscious, you can hide your baldness.' I could say that. For one thing is for sure, if you don't have the guts to accept yourself the way you are, how can you expect others to accept you for who you are?

Baldness in India is like a disease, and those suffering from it are rarely treated with kindness by others. Bullying and body shaming is not considered insensitive either. It is acceptable as a joke shared between many to degrade someone's honour.

I had made my point clear to Rebello by not suggesting anything after being asked. My silence was meaningful. He was actually scared of my audacity, so he didn't expect a reply from me. I too had been a part of an intimidating and rather bullying crowd in my growing-up years.

I don't remember when and how indifference to these things had developed in me. I kept away from talking and gossip mongering on the subject. I had understood that no one deserves to be treated shabbily. But Rebello remained outside this principle of mine and I derived pleasure, silently, from ill-begotten thoughts about his baldness.

3

My aunt used to be a driving force in my childhood. Actually, she was less of a driving force than *some* force. So she existed meaningfully. Period.

She wasn't evil, but she wasn't a saint either. Her ideologies and theories were twisted and aloof.

One evening, as I was returning from school rather earlier than usual, I saw her with a man who was not her husband.

Even through the closed doors I knew that he wasn't my uncle; he sounded like someone else. He was better looking than my sloppy uncle, a man who mostly ignored the presence of my aunt. But he loved and cared for her in his own way. And his way was being loyal. My aunt, on the other hand, was driven by her physical needs. Some days, she would feel guilty and dress up for him so that he would notice her, but he didn't have the drive or the energy. He was sluggish and languid in bed, that's what I assumed from the energy in the house. My aunt could get anyone to come to the house. She was full of energy. Whenever I saw her, I wondered whether love was blind. She was blind for sure.

And the other thing about her was that she never hid her men from me, which meant she felt no shame and embarrassment. And at no point had she felt like I might follow her footsteps; if I did, I think she would be proud. She was comfortable in her sexuality and her needs. Insanely enough, I had also once seen a woman walking out of her room. But that could have been a friendly visit. I never heard voices or anything else when a woman was inside.

My uncle was aware of all these occurrences and he ignored them because he knew he couldn't satisfy my aunt.

They were perfect for each other!

There was an unspoken, unwritten deal between the two. My aunt and uncle maintained commensalism—a one-sided relationship where one of the organisms benefits greatly from the symbiosis. The other is not helped, but it is not harmed or damaged from the relationship either. My aunt, in this manner, was like the cattle egret that feeds on the insects on the cattle's body.

Initially, I used to feel sad for my uncle, but I soon understood their ecosystem. It was not that my aunt did not care for him. She did. She never made fun of him for his inability to satisfy her.

The truth was clear before my eyes. But accepting the truth was more difficult then. We were groomed to believe in love, whether it existed or not, between married couples. We believed that married couples, even when unhappy, had to pretend like everything is fine. Even better if they had kids! They are fertile and inseparable.

No one likes to break through these barriers, these so-called pretensions at civility, to find out the truth. It's a taboo subject in our society.

Looking at my boss, I was reminded of my uncle. He had the same energy my uncle had—docile and inherently deceptive. But my boss was manipulative. It was likely a skill he had acquired at training, or, maybe, at the management school. Management schools teach their students to sit over the other's head and get work done. It doesn't teach you to work in harmony with others. It teaches you to be a leader even when you don't have the capability to be one, and most of the time, the wrong guys become the leaders.

My boss had a management degree and hence, he was the manager. Someone without a degree was not.

It made me think that human beings have automated things to such an extent that they can make animals, even humans, dance at their tunes. I knew, clearly, that there are only a handful of people in the world who drive the rest. The rest like to be driven. They follow norms, make society, live and die. Those handful become bosses.

Sometimes, I think, is all this worth it? Do I want to be driven and be a follower? No!

I could not accept this easily. I was a rebel in my own right.

Sitting there, in his small crabby cabin, body odour perpetually emanating from him, was punishment worse than a death verdict. The piles of papers and files collecting dust on the side of the table made me wonder if anyone actually cleaned the cabin. He had a small fan, but it was greedily positioned towards him. I wondered why he always kept the air-conditioning off in his cabin. Once, when I had asked, he said that according to some religious sage, it's not good for his hormones. It was rumoured that he and his wife had been trying to conceive for a few years and had done away with medical interventions; they had gained confidence while following a goofy-looking Baba. Many believe in him, even though there are no results.

I always let my mind wander whenever I think of the Baba. I already had an image of him in my mind. A guy, sitting on a jewel-studded throne (probably red in colour), closing his eyes while delivering a sermon to the disciples who are gathered around him. I could even see the boss and his wife sitting in front of the Baba, waiting for pearls to fall off from his divine mouth.

My boss typically adhered to whatever he, the Baba, had preached.

Such are our beliefs, or rather, our faith. We don't question things since it is easier to follow and fall prey.

While climbing down the stairs of the call centre tower, I could hear the thunderstorm. The wind was whooshing through small vents and into the building. Water had pooled on the stairs and was flowing through the flashy floors. Winds were pushing the flows through the long lobby.

The lifts had gone out of service and people were rushing down the slippery stairs to evacuate the building as if it were an emergency. Mumbai, the city of dreams, never sleeps and never stops.

This aspect about Mumbai amazed me. People throng from all parts of India to make a name in Mumbai. But most of them face disappointment and hatred because those native to the city are racist. We don't allow anyone to enter our land, and if they do, we crush them and their dreams. We all are the reason behind their failures and sorrows.

The city is a huge, seething mass of humanity. Everyone is happy and sad at the same time.

'Are we indeed civilized?' I wonder.

I have my reservations.

In my memory, this city is always full of people, men, women, boys and girls. More of them. I sometimes think about the many people whom the city has bred, fed and curdled into mockery.

That evening, dark clouds clamoured in the sky. It was as if the gods were at war with each other. I was scared to look directly at the black clouds. It was showering rage. Although I was as scared of the rains, I also wanted to look into its eyes and see pain. I was trying to philosophise thus while walking, but Saira caught up with me, her feet splatting and splashing away.

'How beautiful, isn't it?' she said. She was soft, like she had been made out of cotton balls. I adored how she viewed things, all sunshine and rainbows. I would like to be her, but I couldn't. But one day, I would, I promised myself.

She grabbed my hand and pointed towards the ocean. 'Look, the waves are dancing.'

'Yes, it's the Shiv Tandav!' I said defiantly. I felt a little annoyed by her ignorance. How could she be so oblivious to the fact that it's red-zone weather condition? 'Is she faking?' I thought to myself.

'Rubbish, this happens all the time. Enjoy it while it's here. Tomorrow will be humid and you will wish for rain.'

On second thoughts, I decided to play along. There was nothing to lose. In fact, it was the best idea to hedge my bets on. It could be a survival instinct—fake it till you make it.

We both walked, parallel to the roaring ocean. And walking with Saira did make the walk more pleasurable. The once raging waves now looked like children playing hide-and-seek, waves hiding into the ocean and coming right back to check on you. I quietly thanked god for allowing Saira to be in my life, since she could show me the rainbows and help me waddle through the potholes.

'Hey, do you remember Deva?' she asked while we were enjoying a cup of sweet corn on the streets of Mumbai. We were at Nariman Point, looking at the view of a lifetime. The Queens Necklace looks like a serene pathway to heaven. However, one actually needed to be in heaven to be able to afford a house there. But that thought aside, I was fortunate to work at such a serene location.

'Yes, I know him. That stubby guy, right?' I made a face as I spoke about him. There was something about him that disgusted me. He lacked the same things I lacked and desired in myself. That disgusted me about him.

'I see love in his eyes when he sees you. He is deeply into you.'

Saira was always blunt. She said what she felt, and her first instincts were the only instincts she worked with. She never over- or under-analysed, she only felt. She was a free spirit born into a chained world. In this world of thinkers, she was a believer. Anything she touched, turned into gold. She had some magic in her and some charm as well. It was the sort of spark you hardly found in yourself. I too saw magic in her. In fact, at times, I felt attracted to her. However, early in life I already knew my sexual preferences. One thing was clear to me: I was attracted to men. I wanted a man in my life to pleasure me, though I didn't need one.

Walking on one side of the road, with waves gushing on the other side and the rain splattering around us like a shower of shimmering trinkets, I felt the droplets on my palm. The rain brings memories. Back when I was innocent. Back to college. Once, when it was raining—just like this—as if the clouds had waged a war against Mother Earth.

I took a cab, crouching into that reeking, low, wet seat. It was a relief to get the cab, but the stench made the journey unbearable. I tried to distract myself but my thoughts rushed back to that action that had changed my life forever. I'm sure that everyone who knows me knows about it. Not that I am ashamed, but others make me ashamed. I thought it was natural.

My naivete had got me into situations that were worse enough to have warranted death, but I was made stronger because of them, or so I would like to believe.

My aunt did have an influence on me. I had lied before when I said she had no influence other than that of having existed. I saw that she possessed power around men. I felt like whatever she wanted, she could have. So as I grew, I started emulating her to have the power she had. I craved the attention she got from men.

Plus, this is routine in college. Kids talk about their crushes, attractions, infatuations and rebounds. Their life revolves around these activities, not their studies.

Once, I had the opportunity to be with a football player. In my college, if a person was seen around someone who played a sport, they are then accepted into the cool crowd.

I too wanted that. I wanted to be cool. I wanted to be seen, recognized and accepted. It was raining that day. My soccer-player boyfriend, Shyam, came to me and caught me by my hand. He took me to an empty classroom and started removing my clothes. I hesitated for a moment, but I had opened up to him. So I did as he said. Everything he asked for, I did it to him. I felt like I was his slave, and I wondered whether my aunt would have done the same things. But then, what choice did I have? I was dark-skinned after all and rarely accepted otherwise. So I tried to enjoy it. My eyes were open throughout the whole episode. It was as if I wasn't feeling it. But my aim had been to let him have me, and I had achieved it. I felt like I had won the first prize in some event. I had scored it for life.

I slept like an achiever that night.

I woke up to around a 1,000 messages. Yes, that was it. My act of pride was now a frame for all to view. It had been uploaded on an anonymous site and then further copied to all other platforms possible. That was my name to fame. I was famous! But I was still not accepted.

I still don't know who uploaded it. But I know everyone saw it.

The next day, I saw them staring at me, whispering into

each other's ears. Something that made them giggle made me quiver in fear. My stomach hurt so much that I felt like a thousand pins had been poked into it. Uncontrollable cramps made me crunch into a ball. I was short of breath. I gasped but my body refused to breathe. I opened my mouth to let the air in, but I was dying.

The next few minutes were a blur. I somehow managed to enter the ladies bathroom. I splashed water on my face, but the pain was unbearable. And that's when I had my first meltdown. I collapsed right on the floor, like a dead body.

The other students in the bathroom tried to wake me up, but I was someplace else. A place where I was at peace.

After a few hours, I woke up. I was on a hospital bed. My aunt was sitting on a chair. She was elated to see me awake. Even then, and even now, not once did she ever ask why I did what I did.

I'm jolted back to reality by the soggy seats and the continuously piercing horns of impatient Mumbaikars. Why is this city so angry and so happy at the same time? Mumbai knows no balance.

The cab driver sensed my body language and started speaking to me. 'Madam, no one has any peace of mind here.' He laughed.

I didn't respond but I could feel his pain. 'It must be tough to be on the road the whole day and night, isn't it? With such insensitive people?'

'Not really, some people are very nice. Like you, Madam.'

'Are you new here, Madam?' He clearly was in a mood to chat. It didn't bother me, for a change.

I was taught by my aunt to never reveal my true identity to strangers, so I learned the art of playing along. Storytelling.

'Yes, I am new here. I came from Nepal to this city of dreams. I only have a friend's number.'

The cab driver was now impressed. He was interested in knowing my story. 'Ki, Madam, you don't know anyone here?' he asked, concerned.

'Not really, just a friend.' I gave him bits of information as bait.

'Then what happened, Madam?' His curiosity was now taking over his good senses.

As much as I don't like confusing the innocent, I secretly enjoy it. So I played along, thinking that he too was playing along. It was the usual situation. I defer the guilt by surrendering to my artificial goodness.

'Well, I'll tell you if you tell me about yourself,' I said, sheepishly, diverting attention.

One thing that I've realized is that people love to talk. Give them a chance and they will talk about anything. They love the sound of their own voice and men never decline a lady who is showing interest in them. Their male ego is inflated and a woman can invariably take advantage of that.

'Madam, what can I say? I'm from a small town in West Bengal. My wife and children both have come this year to live with me in Mumbai. My son goes to school. He's in the second standard and argues for more pocket money everyday.'

After a long time, I was reminded of my little cousin brother, a gem of a person.

But suddenly, I had to keep these thoughts to myself. I couldn't believe my eyes.

I was looking straight ahead when I saw Abhi! He was walking with a much older woman. He was holding an umbrella and they were trying hard to stand still without being pushed by the wind. The raging winds didn't spare anyone. I felt a sudden stab of jealousy thinking that the woman could be his wife, though I never bothered to find out Abhi's marital status.

He was among the few others who had decided to walk on the streets at this time. The danger of falling into the potholes was real in Mumbai, many had lost lives and here he was, waltzing away romantically when the city only speaks of fear.

I wondered who she was: his girlfriend, his aunt, his mother, his friend, his soul mate, his colleague. It could be anyone. But I wondered.

'Why do I care?' I thought. He was no one to me. I just knew his name and he only satisfied my desires. Sure, he gave me multiple orgasms. But that's it. He was just a means to an end. But still, I wondered who she was.

Perhaps I could ask him the next time I saw him, but that might sound desperate. Should I stop and offer them a lift? What if he wanted to be left alone and not be seen with her—or rather, with me? Maybe I could text him and ask him if he wanted to hop into the car on this rainy day.

Pushed around by my thoughts, I impulsively rolled the window down and called out to him.

Without much ado, he jumped into the cab with the lady. The lady sat behind, with me, and he sat in the front seat. Somehow, men feel like the seat upfront is for them, like they are responsible for taking care of those behind. And women should sit in the back seat apparently. Otherwise they could be attacked by the cab driver. But hell, men attack men too. Why is that not raised as a concern ever? They should also be sitting in the back seat. How can someone be saved by sitting in the back seat?

They sat on their respective seats and were now in the same boat as me. Soaking wet pants, rainwater getting sucked into the torn leather seats. They were tarnished and mucky too. He looked back at me and gave me a warm smile. Was it a thank-you-for-rescuing-me smile? It clearly wasn't an angry smile.

Was she his girlfriend? Then I asked myself why it bothered me when he was no one to me.

'This is Tanya, my stepmother,' he said.

There was actually no need for an introduction since we meant nothing to each other.

I toyed with the idea of letting my thoughts take flight, consider these things again, but no, I restrained myself. I just let it be.

4

Meera—I wonder why my parents named me Meera. Am I named after Krishna's Meera instead of the radical Meera, the dancer? Whatever the reason, I feel like names have significance. They determine a person. My name produces an identity for those who don't understand me. They see me as the sultry, sexy Meera, or the Sanyasini Meera—like the lustful woman you see in movies, or the meditative idol.

Someone had commented on that scandalous video of mine that had been uploaded on YouTube. 'Which Meera are you?' I remember it vividly. The comment stayed with me, even though the video was removed.

I clearly remember those words, still. They haunt me at night and also console me in days. They build my confidence when I'm high, and break me inside when I'm low. The mind does that to us, makes us believe things are greater than they actually are, and vice versa. Being smart isn't a curse, because then you can reason with all the conclusions and continue reasoning even when the answers are unacceptable. There is never any closure.

While working at my desk, there are times when I feel as if I'm not a part of this universe. I feel free and united with myself. My inner world is a sacred place, and it keeps me sane. Maybe this happens with everyone, or maybe not. However, through it, I can somehow also sense when someone is giving out evil vibes.

Being interrupted when I am in my world annoys me. I do not appreciate it, but I have never told anyone about it. I seem pleasant as a pea when someone does it, but within I'm bothered.

I was interrupted by the handsome Karan.

'Hello!' he said with a wicked smile.

The smile was to die for.

This was new for me. My head was racing. Why was he here? Why was he speaking to me? Did he need me for something? Had I forgotten something? Was I in a parallel universe? Is there something I need to do and haven't…but he wasn't my boss? Was there something we needed to do together? Or worse, had he taken me to be someone else?

I was so lost in my thoughts that I found myself staring at him silently. I was likely to scare him off, but was overwhelmed. So without uttering a word, I kept staring at him. He kept looking at me, not through me, straight at me.

And he was talking to me, which was a rare sight.

'Hello?' I replied, a question colouring my face. 'What could he want from me? Why would he want to interact with me?' After beating myself up trying to decipher the reason behind this summon, I realized I didn't have to think so much. He had surely mistaken me for someone else. As soon as he realized it, he would turn back, never to return. So I just waited there, surprised still.

I was not trying to be a snob, but my body language surely showed signs of disinterest. It was always like this with me. Whenever I am overwhelmed, I make this face, which gives others the impression that I am either uninterested or in a hurry.

This time, too, it looked like I was not interested. Mostly, I think it is better to appear like a snob than to show any compassion, because more often than not, people are conniving. They're up to something and it's always best to give a reaction that's unfavourable.

I have always been a very cautious person, especially after being brought down many times. It just helps my confidence. To fake it till I make it! Showing my vulnerabilities to others was always difficult for me. I'd rather rust in denial than deflower in paradise. It's not my style to sulk over spilled milk, or things that cannot be mine to start with. I look at everything with a suspicious eye and wage bets in any situation. I've burnt my fingers too many times.

I was slowly trying to put my guards up when Karan came closer.

I looked at his smiling face…I could melt into that smile. I wasn't usually someone who got dreamy at every instance, but it was an effect he had. Keeping my cool, I responded with a nod or maybe a shake of the head. I was not sure what that reaction was supposed to convey, but it clearly stood for: what the hell do you need? It was the rudest possible response.

He was still coolly looking at me and smiling. Then he finally broke his silence and spoke. 'My name is Karan, by the way. You are Meera, right?' he exclaimed enthusiastically.

I couldn't believe that he knew my name. He must have heard about my collapsing incident. Maybe someone had told him that I was going to die and he felt bad for me and hence was talking to me. Yes, maybe he had made a resolution to do a good deed for the day and he thought it would make me happy by telling me that he knew my name. I was already trying hard to keep my juggling thoughts under check; just hearing someone new calling my name wreaked havoc in me.

I hated it when I pulled myself down like this, but then again, there was no real explanation as to why he was standing in front of me, acknowledging my name and my presence. I was itching to tell him that I didn't need any sympathy or charity from anyone. I was happy by myself. But that would rush the conversation, and it would be unacceptable in social terms. So I kept quiet, but my mind was racing with loud and clear thoughts.

I had to shut it down. My mind had to stop running for me to be able to listen to this man. Maybe he had something important to tell me.

I said to myself—'Focus, listen to him. Stop talking in your head'—and I looked up at him.

'I have seen you around here but I have never interacted with you before. Thought this would be a good chance to get to know you. Are you new here?' he asked nonchalantly.

New? Me? I wondered what world he was in. I had been here for ages. Had he just noticed me? What? Was he blind? Then I looked down at my breasts to check if they had increased in size to explain his new behaviour, but there was no significant difference, or so I thought. 'Should I ask someone?' I considered, toying the idea in my head.

Somehow, this little conversation had taken over my head. Eternity seemed to pass during this exchange.

All I could do or say was to stare back without blinking.

He might think I am a lunatic but that was my best response to deal with this situation.

I thought that the plastered smile on his face was fake and unmovable. I wondered how it was that some people had a smile stuck on their faces without a hint of emotion. They were like mannequins. He had that same smile. Correct, it was a mannequin smile. Even if you frowned back, you would get the same Barbie-doll smile back. Though he was different from a Barbie.

I had told myself to shut up a million times already, but my mind was still talking, and the thoughts were louder now.

'I have been here even before you. Maybe I should ask you if you are new here?'

Swoosh! My comment went right through him, through his plastered smile and I saw him falter. 'Mission accomplished! I have made someone feel bad about themselves today. That seems to be my mantra for the year after all,' I thought.

I stood there now, calmer, waiting for him to reply, which he was quick to do.

'I am not very social so I only communicate with my department. So then you are my senior here. Maybe we can go grab a coffee at the cafeteria to get to know each other.'

And he put that plastered smile back on.

Now I was growing suspicious. What did he want from me? And as direct as I always was, I went right ahead and asked.

'What do you want? You don't need to spend time with me to ask for a favour. Go right ahead, I'll do what I can.' I spoke as is my nature. That was my superpower. I could be brutally honest even when it was unnecessary. And the sparkle in my eyes was unmissable; it was as if I had won an award or something with my comment.

'Well there is nothing I want, but now I'm surely intrigued by you.' With his smile fading, he seemed more like a human being—someone with whom perhaps I could interact.

And then, I thought, 'What the hell!'

'Sure! How about after lunch? At 4 p.m.? We can meet for coffee.'

I was quick to make decisions but I still wondered what a 27-year-old man would want from a 34-year-old lady. 'Maybe he wanted to have a one-night stand? Maybe he knew I had sex with strangers for fun. Maybe he was a serial killer. Maybe he…'

I had to stop thinking till it was time. I didn't do much work till lunch. I had a lot to do but I kept wondering what Karan had wanted. Then thoughts of scenarios crossed my mind and I then tried to grasp at what I, Meera, could do in the scenarios. I never assumed that he just wanted an innocent friendship.

As usual, I think of the worst. Hence, the worst happens.

After lunch with Saira, I forgot all about the coffee date.

I only remember what's pleasant—something that has zapped out my energy, those encounters I tend to forget. I've always worked on this skill as a kid and have gained experience over the years. I don't just push the encounters under the carpet, I erase it from my memory.

It was time.

'Hey there!' shouted Karan.

It annoyed me when people acted so affable. Something seemed off. It was too fake to be real, but I played along. I was waiting and watching his moves.

We went ahead and grabbed our cups of coffee, and he immediately signalled me to join him, to the terrace. The smoking zone. We walked to the terrace and there were some other smokers there as well. The smoking zone was never empty; there was always a smoker or two there. It's funny how smokers start relating to each other; they share cigarettes and matches and lighters. It's a great community to be a part of—like meeting your own. A lot of business meetings are held here and a lot of promotion promises are made here. Non-smokers don't know what they are missing—sometimes they miss out on new assignments too. But still, I would like to alert everyone with the usual statutory warning: smoking is injurious to health.

There he was! That portly boss of mine, Rebello. I didn't know, nor had I ever tried to know whether my boss was a smoker. Finding him on the terrace surprised me. I took it in my stride and remained unmoved.

Karan lit my cigarette first and then his own.

Seeing Rebello around made me conscious while I was

smoking. I only hoped that he wouldn't think that I had a thing with Karan. Not that it mattered to anyone. It wasn't anyone's business.

'So where are you from?' he asked with his characteristic smile again.

I had to address the elephant in the room so I gunned for it. 'What do you want from me? Is there something you want to tell me? Do you think I'm a lunatic? Did you hear about me fainting in the office the other day? What have you heard about me? Do you know something about me and want to talk about that? Do you think my breasts have become bigger suddenly?'

Out of breath, I finally looked up at him. His smile had vanished and now he looked scared. I felt bad for him immediately after the volley of questions. I had tried to scare him off with my crazy behaviour. Clearly, I found some sadistic happiness in doing so.

Then, on a whim, I looked up at him with a plain expression, as if nothing had happened. I tried to read his expression. By now, he had somewhat adjusted to my insanity.

He now seemed nervous when he tried to speak. He had a premonition about my replies.

But somehow, we managed to overcome the initial hitches and struck up a conversation.

And then, we actually hit it off.

Soon enough he started calling me 'Jogan Meera' and I named him 'Bichara Karan'. We usually had a hearty laugh over this. Karan played the 'Bichara card' quite well. I too had dropped off all my pretenses.

All this while, I had been secretly working with Rebello on the project. Since it was confidential, I did not share it with anyone—neither with Saira nor with Karan. The work was going fantastically. I didn't think I would enjoy working on this as much as I actually was. It was new and exciting, and most importantly, it was not overshadowed by anyone else—no one who was phony, or looking to impress the bosses by being an ass-licker just to get a promotion.

It amuses me when I see someone working only for increments or promotions. It's like they don't want to invest in themselves and their own creative bursts. It's weird that no one sees the correlation—if they work harder then they will creatively uplift themselves, which may or may not provide them tangible gains but it will surely give them the solace of being true to their own skills and utilising them to the fullest. I was not looking for anything from this project. I wasn't looking for recognition either. All that I hoped for was that the new branch would turn out perfectly and be much more effective than the current one. I had immense faith in myself and, therefore, I never tried to take shortcuts to make it big.

I was also aware that the reason Rebello had taken me on this project was because he knew I wasn't ambitious. In fact, I was the opposite of ambitious. If I worked on something, I'd rather die than present it in a meeting. And hence, he had always flourished in my existence. He got promotions after promotions.

Initially, he thought that I would be elated about salary hikes, but he soon realized that nothing motivates me.

Nothing but creative bursts, especially in a call centre job since the monotony kills you. So he took advantage of that situation.

He knew I was smart. He also knew that because of my circumstances, I couldn't go to the best college and get the best degree. The degree is the only thing one notices in a resume. His calculating mind had seen through my situation and now, while working on the project, he was reassured about my disaffection. He might have been happy that he could now use my calibre for his schemes. Usually, people don't even get an interview if they don't match the minimum qualifications. So yes, I was aware that I couldn't be a part of the rat race or climb the ladder. So, I made an announcement to myself. 'Don't try to reach it,' I told myself.

At the office, I cultivated an aura of mystery around me and let no one penetrate it. This proved to be extremely helpful since I was alone in the city and it helped me keep people at bay. And this also gave them ample freedom to judge me, make scandals about me and spread canards about me. I was not bothered.

As time passed, I realized that I was distracted with Karan. Now, he wanted to go for frequent tea breaks. Then he wanted to have lunch dates, dinner dates, and even wanted to get to know me better.

It was an extraordinary feeling when I realized that someone wanted to know me! I always felt that I was above all these expectations. But Karan came into my life like a waft of fresh breeze.

I slowly started giving in.

5

The dew was a smudge on the window. It was raining outside and our strong, deep, passionate breaths inside the room made it hard to breathe. But I couldn't get myself away to catch a breath, and he kept coming on to me, like a roaring lion. He stuck his head between my breasts and nibbled on them, gently and slowly rubbing his tongue around my nipples, hardening them with every twirl his tongue took around them. Every time he finished a twirl, he would suck up one nipple, and as he saw it hardening, I could feel him hardening too. He grew bigger and bigger with every stroke of his tongue. At times he had to stop because he was moaning. He moved between both the breasts masterfully, which gave him and me pleasure beyond words.

And then, suddenly, he stopped. It was as if he was possessed or had a depressing thought or he had remembered something. Perhaps something I did made him retreat but something was wrong. His face went red and he was unable to speak. He was lost in a thought so deep and so disturbing that his expressions changed. *'What could it be!'* I wondered but all I knew about this naked man next to me was his name. Nor did I want to know him any better—I'd have to repeat that to myself all the time. This was the unsaid rule: that neither of us wanted to have deeper connections. He was least interested in me.

I often had the urge to ask him questions but he was usually distant, he lacked any external interest in me. He reached for my blouse without even looking at me. Had he always been so disturbed, or does he show this side of himself to me alone? They say that you show your worst side to your closest alliances. Was this his way of thanking me for accepting him? As twisted as it could be, it made sense.

Drawn as I was to Abhi sexually, I was equally in awe of Karan. I liked the way he treated me, the way he wanted to spend time with me to know me. No one had ever done that with me before this. It was hard to believe in the current scenario. And I knew he wanted something more, but what was it? What he could ask for bothered me a lot. But more often than not, I just wanted to bask in the glory of believing that someone wanted me for me.

Since my childhood, I had convinced myself that I was not lovable. Karan was defying that notion in my head and slowly in my heart too.

Walking into the glass office today felt like my life had changed altogether. Someone was waiting for me in the office, someone other than Saira. Someone wanted me. I walked in with renewed love for myself. Karan had already messaged me to say that he was waiting for me on the terrace.

I always thought there were better things in life than

being loved, or liked. You could be spiteful or mean or edgy. I never advocated for falling in love just because one needed to love someone.

The most extravagant, gorgeous things and people were around us. It's up to us to find them.

I wasn't the butterflies-in-my-stomach kind of person. I was a dry, practical, pathetic, self-pitying character. One who had been dropped into this fairy tale and was unable to react in an appropriate manner. I didn't know the protocols of being in love—or even how to react when you are being appreciated or noticed by anyone. Attention made me uncomfortable. This interest was doing wonders for me, but all I thought of was love. Sure, I was broken, but I wasn't a pessimist. I too wanted to believe in love and the feeling of love.

Karan had come into my life at a time when I was mentally more stable. I made fewer issues out of nothing and was almost at peace with myself.

So here I was. I stood in front of my true love—Lord Shiva. I was praying to him and trying to reason why he had brought about a situation like this. There was someone who liked me, who showed love towards me. It would only bring out expectations that I had buried deep inside.

My current dilemma was real and had to be addressed. After all, every time I saw a couple in love, did I not ridicule them because I don't believe in love?

Now Shiva was testing my strength and commitment towards my convictions. I have always visited this Lord Shiva temple since my childhood. I have prayed with all my heart. I have told him things that I haven't said to anyone else.

He was the father I didn't have and sometimes the sister I wished for. Now, after so many years of protecting me, he wanted to touch my heart with love.

I would and could take this challenge and show him how I could stay, or come out of this unscathed.

'I won't let anything affect me,' I promised. I said it to myself and prayed I was right and could live up to my ideals.

However, I had to get up and move to meet Karan—my date. Yes, I was officially on a date with Karan. As much as possible, and without any expectations, I would like to enjoy it.

This was not my first date, but it was a date after ages. I couldn't remember the last time I had a date with anyone or felt something for anyone. It wasn't that I felt that elusive feeling now.

But I was trying. Because as much as I tried to deny it, I could feel a tingling in my bones—not love, not passion, just anticipation. Anticipation of the unknown that awaited me.

I put my best outfit on. For another woman, it would have seemed like a simple everyday outfit placed on a lanky body. But I felt beautiful.

There were rare occasions when I felt beautiful. Men do, and have been interested in my body, but Karan wanted to go to dinner with me. How absurd was that! In my head such a scenario could not come to pass, not with such a handsome man and with such a desire.

I floated out of my apartment in my short black dress, with a pair of dainty dangling earrings and high heels. I walked into my Uber in waiting. I noticed a few men staring at me, but it felt different today. It felt nice.

What was Karan igniting within me? If I didn't see him for one day I would be left with a feeling of helplessness. He was probably the first man to treat me with love...or at least respect? *'Should I jump into this wishing well?'*

With thoughts like these and no awareness of where I was going, I continued my journey en route. I continually kept peeping in the car mirror to see how I looked. The driver, like any other driver, tried to check me out. It disgusted me and I got off the cab at the destination with a frown.

I had never been to this part of Mumbai. Kamala Mills. It was an Italian restaurant—the talk of the town, just launched and was in the news every day. Celebrities walked in and out of the restaurant like it was a public park. It was a new place to hang out; a new place to be clicked and seen. I wondered why anyone would want to be seen. Isn't it always better to be quiet and do your job?

As I walked into the restaurant I took deep breaths. 'In and out,' I repeated to myself to stay calm. My anxieties were rising and I considered whether I should just return home. The confidence I had felt was now being replaced by a huge lump in the throat along with a burning sensation in the gut. I was tense, I realized. Then, instantly, there was a shift and I loosened up again.

'No, Meera no! This isn't the time to be childish,' I told myself. And soon enough, I was sweating again.

As I was about to abort this mission, I felt a hand tap my shoulder. As I turned around, I saw Karan standing beside me—way too close for my comfort. He was almost breathing in my nervousness.

'Wasn't I supposed to feel good about his proximity?' But I didn't enjoy it. I took a step back and almost fell a step behind. Again, I was being paranoid. Here was a man trying his best to come closer to me, and here I was, stepping away like he smelled bad.

He was there, right there! Here was Karan, in flesh and blood! So lovely, vibrant and full of promises. I knew he was propitious. I have probably waited for someone like him for all these years.

'Get your act in line, Meera,' I murmured to myself.

I managed a faint smile. He came closer and kissed my cheek and said, 'You look gorgeous!'

I felt his lips on my skin and his strong musky cologne blew me away. I felt it within me. I loved being touched, much like anyone else. He held my hand and walked me to the restaurant.

The place had exquisite decor. The floor was clad with chestnut brown wooden flooring and shimmering white lilies were painted on the ceiling over a background of starlight in blue and pale white. The layout was that of a maze. The bar was bustling with energetic bartenders making mojitos and martinis. Some guests were hanging out at bar stools, chatting away and laughing merrily. The host walked us to a corner of the room to a table for two. As I walked I noticed that the floor had laser lighting randomly placed at different paths to make it look like a labyrinth. The wooden table was shaped like a sphere. The round chairs looked odd in the setting.

I personally believe that a little time spent in a business meeting or at a pub is enough to reveal some elementary human truths. Primarily that we all are fake most of the time. We congratulate an arch rival on a triumph while choking inside. We become cordial even to crashing bores. Similarly, at a pub we don't mind exchanging warm smiles with our ex, or shaking a leg with those who have knocked us down.

Karan pulled out a chair for me like a gentleman. Again I thought, 'What does he want from me?' But I brushed it aside. I knew Karan to be quite chivalrous.

I smiled and sat down, trying to calm my nerves.

'What would you like to drink?'

We both settled down with a bottle of white wine. Ideally, I could calm down with a few shots of tequila. But this was good enough—he had even offered to share a bottle. I wondered how he could afford this. I had suggested a cheaper place but he had insisted, saying that it was his treat, so I tagged along. No way would I splurge at a place like this myself. And I wasn't embarrassed to say that I couldn't afford it. I was comfortable in my skin to say that.

Today, it was the alcohol that made me feel comfortable.

Surprisingly, while I was still on my first glass, Karan was already on his third. Without making much fuss, we decided to order our food.

'I'd like to get the buratta entrée and a mushroom burger along with it,' I said.

Karan looked at me like I was joking. He begged me to order more food. Shutting him down, I said that it would be more than enough for me. And immediately, I felt like I shouldn't have. Confrontation wasn't my forte, especially in a date-like scenario. I usually ran from it.

He raised his hand up in the air and smiled at the waiter. The waiter gave him a knowing smile and came around. Karan was a very charming person. I realized I had somehow not looked at Karan properly, so far. I stared. He looked absolutely handsome. Dressed in dark blue denim and black shirt, he looked like a guy right out of a *Playboy* magazine.

I had noticed it at the office as well, but today he had upped his game. He was kind and courteous to the waiter (unlike many others who focused on impressing their dates). If I looked closer, he appeared comely. He was actually dressed in a slovenly but picturesque way, his hair flying about in all directions.

As Karan got busy talking to the waiter, I thought about the waiter's job. 'It must be a hard job being a waiter, listening to everyone banter all day. But I guess, a job for extroverts would exhaust an introvert.'

'Anything more, Sir?' The waiter's voice brought me back to the present.

'Yes! I'll take one more bottle of wine. My lady here has drunk only one glass and I want her to enjoy her evening. In case she needs some more, we should have it,' saying this, he looked at me and flaunted a charming smile.

I had considered that he was trying to get me drunk, but now I was convinced of the fact. I chuckled discreetly. The wine would colour my inner world.

'And I will eat...' There was a brief pause as Karan was going through the menu. Once done, he said, 'I will have endive salad, burrata salad, potato wedges...' He paused again and the waiter was about to leave.

'Abe Ruk!' he says out loud. 'I will also order the main course.'

The waiter was unmoved but I was amazed and a little shocked. I had started to enjoy the whole thing. Karan was quite zealous after downing some pegs and I was feeling high looking at him.

'Double cheese chicken burger and cheese arabiatta,' he said finally.

I looked at him in disbelief. No wonder he had seemed so offended when I had decided on what to order. This man was a monster, I thought.

I thought it wasn't fair to judge. But soon enough, I couldn't stop myself. He chomped like a monster, he swallowed his meat and didn't chew it. He reminded me of Kumbhkaran, the giant who only ate and slept. But Karan seemed to love every bit of his meal. It was a game for all that he did, drank and ate like he had to win. I knew, after all, that I was on a date. Karan had taken me out on a date.

The Meera I was today was a different Meera. I didn't recognize her. She laughed and giggled and blushed. She loved the praises he showered on her, even though she didn't believe them—in that moment it made her feel happy and loved. She believed that she deserved love. This Meera was a happy Meera. Happiest moments are rarely planned. They're predestined. We don't need to try so damn hard.

I liked *this* Meera. For the first time in many years, I went home and fell asleep soundly. I slept without the sounds from an app or a documentary. It was indeed a good night's sleep after a long, long time. On other nights, I stood uselessly on the balcony, watching the dark sky or the boat-shaped moon. The windless, sultry nights sometimes brought back the memories of my childhood. I was in denial today. Today, I had simply enjoyed the night, the time spent together with Karan, the alcohol and the camaraderie. It had felt like a complete package.

Running was usually therapeutic for me. I needed it most mornings, if not all. Today was a special day. I woke up, feeling fresh as a flower and wanting to take over the world. The world that had seemed daunting yesterday seemed within my grasp.

I had yoga on my to-do list as well. I went to my balcony where I spread my grey yoga mat and did pranayama. I usually loved the cool morning breeze on my face and the rising sun while practising yoga. It always brought me new hopes.

I kept reminiscing about the last evening. How Karan had touched my hand while talking. The way he had looked into my eyes. What he had said and how he had said it so gently. There is magic when someone talks to you while looking right into your eyes, and that too still smiling like an idiot. Yes, there surely was magic in his eyes.

I got dressed and went for a run. I circled around so many people during my run. They were all different but still the same. Human nature is constant after all. Little did I know that people are all unique, each like none other.

There were a couple of men and women in their late fifties who were chatting and galloping around the magnificent neem tree that kept showering them with blessings by shedding its dry leaves. It was an awe-inspiring sight that morning. I looked at everyone and felt that they believed in life and were enjoying it. Everything seemed beautiful this morning. The Brahma Kamals looked exotic, like always, but today, they were especially romantic and blooming like never before. Even the fishermen and their bickering wives made the purchases seem hilarious. Nothing was perturbing me this morning—not the sun, not even the rain. Surely the adrenalin was playing a game with my mind.

Later, while running, I was listening to Shiva Stotram when my phone buzzed with a message.

It was Karan. 'Good morning, beautiful!' he said, adding a heart-swoosh emoji. My heart skipped a beat. It came in like a bolt from the blue. I almost tripped on the pipe watering the small lawn facing the sea. I wanted to scream and shout out in joy, but I maintained my composure.

However, while walking into the apartment building, I was reminded of my real life.

I saw Abhi on his balcony. I knew why he was standing there. I also knew that he had seen me returning in the night from my date. I was dressed to kill. Maybe he knew or could have guessed. Then a saner thought came to my mind. 'Who is he to judge? Isn't he a married man himself?'

But it brought me back to reality, and reality always bites. He looked at me with anticipated longing in his eyes. His bloodshot red eyes looked as if they had been fantasising about me since last night, when he had noticed a happier Meera in that dress, glowing with joy.

He seemed like he was waiting to kill my happiness.

The mind is a manipulative machine. One day it makes

you think that someone is a saint and at some other moment, that same person seems like a monster. The truth is that no one is a saint or a monster. It's the moment that is evil or good—not the person. Situations and circumstances are to be blamed, if we have to blame someone at all. Yes, there are innate qualities that drive people to behave in a particular manner, but still we can train our minds and fix negative attributes. Time is key to be able to do this. You can be an angel and a devil in the same lifetime, and to the same person at different times.

I was feeling that way towards Abhi.

He looked uglier than usual to me today. It could be my internal turmoil or my guilt at having gone out with someone else. But there had never been any relationship between us. It was just sex and our physical needs. As per Maslow's hierarchy of needs, i.e. at the very peak of Maslow's hierarchy are the needs of self-actualisation. And sex is one of the important needs. All he has done is to satisfy that need. I argued with myself in my head. I also tried to justify my feelings.

I remembered reading somewhere, 'No woman gets an orgasm from shining the kitchen floor.' So I should feel no regrets about having sex with Abhi.

I brushed the bad thoughts aside and lay on the bed after the run.

I understood that soon Karan would conquer my mind and heart. I would not like to carry any emotional baggage of my fling with Abhi. I had already trained my mind to tow the line, to move the way my heart felt and I saw no problem from Abhi's side regarding this.

Life moved on between my office, runs and Karan. Slowly, everything around me was covered in a fresh hue of love. I did not resist it. It was allowed to come and touch my life. It was all I wanted from life. It was what I deserved.

Karan had spread through my life like water in a colour palette—the more he spread his influence, the more colourful the palette became.

We took to each other like the river and the bank. We were constantly touching, feeling, at times breaking, but being constant with the other. Our worlds fused—one with the other—and a dam broke in me. I found my real sky outside the canvas of my earlier life. Probably, Karan too discovered the meaning of his own life.

6

It was our six-month anniversary. Yes, I officially had a boyfriend now. 'Meera has a boyfriend,' I said. It felt weird in my head when I heard it. But it was true. I was still not sure how I felt about it. What I wanted to make of it.

But when I walked into the office, I felt that I loved myself more. It was because someone said that he liked me. His charm was hypnotising.

As each day passed, I was seeing a change in my behaviour. I was growing dependent on him.

The sane part of me kept telling me that I should not give in to someone so completely, but my heart said I should dive right in. But other thoughts crowded as well. 'What will I do if I do not know how to swim? What will happen if I drown? Will I die?' I thought I would. Even if I don't love, I will still die. I would still live even if I failed in love. I would float like a lifeless leaf, but I would float and not drown. I knew myself. I knew that I was a great survivor.

Perhaps I would rise to the occasion, like I have in other adverse situations. I've always risen above situations with my grit and determination. Now too I would rise if I needed to. I wouldn't hesitate if the need arose.

But I am a human too and have emotions.

The fear of being deserted always forced me to take shit lying down, especially as a child. But now I was not crippled by it anymore. The people who had once mattered in my life did not bother to know my heart or my mind. Most times, people rejected me for telling the truth. I grew up with the pain of being deceived. I was the talk of the town, but that was hardly a death threat.

Now that I was a self-sufficient woman, abandonment no longer meant the end of my life.

This was karma. I now actually had someone who liked me and wanted me for me.

I donned a sparkling smile and walked towards the cafeteria where Karan was waiting for me. And again, my mind wanted to find reasons to not be in this state of dreamy love. Currently, I was like a rudderless ship, aimlessly drifting towards unknown shores.

Watching him eat, I thought again, 'Why does he swallow his food? Don't normal people just chew and eat? Why does he have to eat enough for four people? Hasn't he heard of eating in moderation…his mouth is always open while eating. Stop talking, eat first.'

I paused. It felt like my thoughts had been loud enough for him to hear and he closed his mouth.

Where had the unflinching, man-slaying, borderline rude Meera gone? I was acting differently with him. I didn't like the different me, but I turned into another person around him. Karan had spelt his charm over me. He was surely a magician!

Then the whole idea of being bedazzled and not in control of my own actions seemed beguiling and a little eerie too. I remembered hearing about magic acts where the audience had become hypnotised as they watched what the magician was doing on the stage. I felt as if I was in the audience and Karan was the magician on the stage. It seemed spooky to lose my mind in this way.

With all the internal dialogues going on, I glanced upon Saira. I saw the disgust in her eyes. Even after having spent some time with Karan, Saira wouldn't stop nagging me about him. She could not stand him. I did not stop her nor did I feel bad about her views. I remained unconcerned about her opinion.

Saira didn't know we were in a relationship. We'd gotten serious a few months earlier. We had just confessed our love to each other. Then, the very next day at the office, as soon as Karan saw me, he turned away. A cold shrug was all I got.

I felt perplexed and thought that he hadn't seen me.

Of course, I understood that he wanted to keep our relationship private but it hurt. It still hurts now. Now, as I think about it, that shrug said a lot without saying anything. There was a hidden meaning to it, a connotation. Words, after all, were a blanket to real meaning. We have to dig in to find the essence.

I always believed that Karan was befriending me to achieve something that I had and he wanted. Now that could be anything: my body, mind or soul. I wondered if he truly had such larger manipulative aspirations, but looks can be deceitful.

All throughout this internal dialogue in my brain I could hear the background noise of aggressive chewing and munching. Sometimes my dreams had the same background score—repetitively. I decided to tell him about it, but I was not sure if I could muster the guts to tell him that I hated the way he ate.

There are a few things I had learned about myself over these six months of being with Karan. Some of these I was not too proud of, and some I took pride in.

I had always thought that I wasn't capable of being in a relationship with anyone and now I had proved myself wrong. I didn't think that I was lovable and it turned out that I could be loved. I didn't believe I could let someone have such hold on me. I have been scared at every step in this relationship. I believed that I didn't deserve love and there would be a breaking point, and this feeling lingered. I think it will continue. I only loved myself, I used to think. But here, in this relationship with Karan, I did not feel connected to him, I just loved him because he said he loved me.

There were many times when I felt the pressure to perform, more than my comfort would allow. I dreaded the day this relationship would end, but I dreaded the slow death of the relationship more. I believed that the end was imminent.

I still woke up thinking that this was a dream.

And so much more passed through my mind.

Saira was at her limit. 'I don't know why you insist on being with chunky Karan. He disgusts me. Next time he eats with us, I'm leaving.'

Saira needed to know and I wanted to tell someone.

'I'm seeing him,' I said softly, as though it was top secret information that needed to be handled delicately.

Her eyes widened in utter disbelief.

'What?' She paused. 'Karan?' She looked baffled. I couldn't read her. All I saw was she was stunned.

'Meera, he is a male chauvinist pig! Why would you date him? And what about your innocent, creative neighbour?'

I was suddenly taken aback. 'How does she know?'

She noticed the effect of her words and immediately said, 'I know things about you that even you don't. No offense.' She smirked.

Saira scared me at times. I loved her to bits but her intuitive power was freakish.

'Why, why?' she repeated. Saira needed time to get over this shock that I had given her.

I looked at her with puppy eyes. I wanted her to accept him.

'You are already behaving out of character, Meera. He isn't for you! Deep inside you know and hence you are turning to me for validation. But I can't be blinded by your changed attitude. Remember, if your guards are down with him, he will eat you up and change you completely.'

I continued pleading with my eyes and immediately I caught myself. I was not acting like my usual self. I was being naive.

But of course, Saira gave in and hugged me.

That evening, I met Karan at a beach side cafe. He was

sitting at the rear end of the cafe—hidden, easily missed by most passers-by, doting eyes on me and only me. Every time he looked at me, I saw passion like I'd never seen before. The love in his eyes made me wonder and question. But I also drowned right into those eyes. I too had the same look when I saw him, I thought. The 'madly in love' looks. They were lusty and romantic at the same time.

I fell right into his arms with those eyes.

He pulled my chair closer to his own as I sat there, dreamily lost in the love in his eyes. The breeze was merciless; my hair blew right on my face as he kissed me passionately, like no one was looking. I used to feel embarrassed when he kissed me in public, but I have gradually gotten addicted to it. I longed for those passionate, long kisses, no matter where we were.

I felt like I was his prisoner in love. Yes, I was addicted to him.

Soon, he was engrossed in his phone. He was messaging and chatting with someone. He was always distracted while he was on his phone. Sure, he gave me a lot of attention, but once past holding hands and kissing or anything physical, he drifted apart. He wasn't someone who talked sweet nothings into my ears. But to my luck, I wasn't like that either. However, if I was being honest, I was actually moulding myself to be more like what he was.

Soon my phone beeped. It was Mr Rebello. He needed me in the office. I bid Karan good-bye and was about to leave when he held my hand.

'Who was it?' he asked rather curtly.

Masking my distaste at the tone with a fake smile, I replied, 'Office.'

I hadn't told him about the project I was working on. It was confidential and moreover, it never came up. And today, his attitude made it harder for me to tell him. So I just shrugged and ignored his boorishness.

It felt soothing. It wasn't very out of my character but felt like I was revolting.

I started gathering all my belongings from the table, antagonistically and dramatically. It was comical because all I had to gather was my phone and a file. In hindsight, I think I was looking for my self-respect on the table. I seemed to be forgetting around this man.

'Where are you going?' he asked again. 'Maybe I can join you.' Seeing me like this, agitated, he was now calming down. He always had such a passive aggressive attitude when he saw me showing my nature, which was an angry one at present. He backed off. At times he made me feel foolish for overreacting because he would just take a 180-degree turn.

This put the blaze out but I was still disturbed by his behaviour. I wanted to hold my ground and not tell him where I was going.

'I'm agitated by the tone of your voice. It's better we don't talk about where I was going and refrain from talking about such things in future.'

Clearly our relationship had moved past the stage where we adored each other so much that we ignored the ugly parts. Now I saw through his acts and he saw through mine.

I was being immature and foolish but what could I do

in a situation where I was torn between my wit and heart. Sometimes his arguments and behaviours were strange. But I wondered whether he ever meant what he said. He surely came across as a modern, liberal gentleman, but deep inside he was very laid back and old-fashioned. Not that old-fashioned is bad, but he did have ideas that would be ridiculed in this modern agnostic world of ours.

I started walking out. But he held my waist and pulled me back and kissed me passionately. That was my weakness. His kisses made me drool, almost made me his slave. He intertwined his fingers into mine like they belonged there. He moved his fingers into the back of my shirt, swirling his fingers into circles—casting a spell on me. His circling motions grew, then decreased. The rhythm of his fingers made me itch and twitch.

But this time I would not give into his seductive moves and I wouldn't let him get away with this unruly behaviour. I pulled his hand out of my back and simply tucked my chin under my shirt. He backed off. His expression changed and I walked away.

The next day at work I didn't look at him, didn't go to the terrace for my usual coffee and smoke either. Saira was surprised that I wasn't clinging on to him like a magnet, like I always did. And something different happened. I was in a meeting with Mr Rebello when Deva walked in. He was to be a part of this confidential project we were working on. My nerves were already on edge and seeing him aggravated me.

'What are you doing here?' I asked him curtly and suddenly repented for having been so rude. Counting my breaths in and out, I calmed my nerves. I gave a meek smile and Mr Rebello announced, 'He too will be working with us on this project.'

Deva was eager, and he was more than elated to work with me. Since he had seen me in the office, he wouldn't stop looking and staring. Something about me probably made him feel calm. Deva was nervous around people and at times, he would become tongue-tied. He grew anxious in meetings with big numbers and many times, he even succumbed to the pressure. He was made fun of when he spoke. Even though he had the ideas, he wouldn't raise them because he knew he would be embarrassed by his colleagues.

I had always been his secret crush, I knew, but he hadn't told anyone about it. Of course, I personally felt like he was looking over my shoulder.

The three of us sat down and I could feel his eyes on me. Mr Rebello too sensed something out of the ordinary, but the boss didn't really care. He went along with what he saw and heard. He was not intuitive, to say the least.

The meeting was odd in the beginning, but as I listened to Deva, I grew interested. I had not imagined that he could have a head over his shoulders. He clearly was an underdog and I knew that Mr Rebello was good at identifying the underdogs and using them to his advantage. Rebello could find a gold mine and keep it hidden, he even had the knack of dulling someone's shine.

I sat over coffee with him at the cafeteria and Saira joined us. She was pleasantly surprised to see us together.

'Hey, since when have the two of you started hanging

out?' She looked clearly at me and glanced over Deva, as if making sure who he was.

Sometimes I wished I was like Saira and said what I thought. I wish I just poured the thoughts out without processing them inside my head a million times, before saying it. I envied that skill.

Looking at her, adamantly waiting, I knew she wouldn't leave without extracting an answer.

But I tried. 'Why don't you sit down with us?'

I liked the suspense, and clearly Deva didn't feel obliged to answer either. He was sipping his coffee like he was in a coffee shop with some strangers.

I eyed Saira and tried to divert the conversation, but she sat right next to me and began to talk to Deva. He was now refusing to react to her presence.

'So, Mr Deva, the whole office thinks you can't talk. Can you? Let's hear you talk.'

He looked up right at her face and said, 'I don't talk to everyone and anyone.' And then, he paused for some time and continued. 'And not everyone wants to talk to me.' He looked into his coffee while saying that, as if he was looking for some dirt in it. His tone had been withdrawn, almost dismissive. He looked out over the cup and beyond. He then wrapped a greyish coarse shawl around his shoulders to beat the considerable cold. I marvelled at the fact that he looked exactly the same, like the interruption hadn't happened at all or it had, leaving him wholly unaffected.

Saira immediately felt regretful about her behaviour. It was the way he had spoken, even I felt a pinch of pain.

However, Saira tilted her head and smiled at him, a warm smile. One that she had never given Karan. Karan always got the vilifying look.

'Here, why don't you try some doughnuts?'

And just like that, he was allowed into her sanctuary. I mean Saira was no rock star but her criteria for allowing entry of people into her lives was complicated. It was a critical and arduous line to cross over.

Witnessing this interaction made me doubt my choices. Karan was still someone she hated. 'I don't see why you can't make friends like Deva instead of Karan. Karan is full of fake arguments and misogyny. I don't see what has attracted you to him. All he has is a pretty face. There's a devil residing within,' she would say. She was a better judge of people, and she chose me when no one wanted to be around me. But I was tightly clasped in Karan's claws.

The sunset was magnificent from the cafeteria where we were sitting. I was facing the sun. I watched the golden hues that formed on the silvery water of the roaring ocean. It looked like a golden stream was heading towards us and then disappearing somewhere in between. The sea united with the smaller waves and calmed itself down into smaller pieces. This cohesion was true to its being and natural at its best. Deva was looking right at me, over the golden rays. When he looked at me, I felt beautiful. I could feel my bronze skin shining through his eyes. Saira's interruption distracted his reverie.

'This sun is hitting my face. Deva, go get a glass of water,' Saira said. She bossed everyone around, and that was another reason why she didn't like Karan; he too liked to boss people around.

Deva was obviously dumbfounded but he went and got her a glass of water. She intimidated him, but I knew she liked him. She was a bully. And he got a glass for me too. I got up to leave and so did Deva. It was as if he was my pet dog.

I was surprised to realize that I liked it.

'Would you be walking to the train station?' he asked.

I nodded and he sprinted to his desk to grab his lunch bag. He then stood next to me. Yes, now it was confirmed that I had earned myself a loyal pet. An ugly dog. I hated my thoughts sometimes, but I've learned to embrace them as mine.

The sun had completely set and the moon was shining. A few stars appeared around the rusty bronze sun. The stars, as they made their way into the night, were a sight.

On a path that cut through a woody bush, I walked on and he followed me. He was slower and I almost lost sight of him in the dark maze. The backwaters had receded to a sluggish stream where the mouth had silted up. The place is deserted, mournful, I thought. No birds twitter. No cattle graze. There was the slow, sad, rush of a cold wind. There were some roughly hewn-out stone steps I stopped for a minute and then chose to hurry up. Deva followed me like an obedient pup.

Deva had so much to say it amazed me. He was like a small kid. He spoke about his family, which was my weak streak. I missed having a loving, caring family.

'You are lucky to have a family waiting back at home for you,' I told him despondently.

He empathised with my pain but this was the most I could share. He surprised me. I wouldn't have said something like this to anyone, not Karan, not even myself.

And then, I was interrupted by a message. Karan. 'Meet me @ mocha?'

I searched for a heart emoji or an apology, but the tone in which I read it in my head made me feel like not answering it. I looked back at Deva and he smiled like a gentle giant.

At the station he asked me if I wanted some juice, I refused. I smiled while leaving, touching his shoulder briefly. His face lit up at that.

On my way home, I tried to process my feelings towards Deva but I wasn't sure. So I turned to the radio and heard my favourite RJ bantering about the traffic. An easy way out! That night I didn't even reply to Karan's 'goodnight' message!

The next day, I walked through the hallway and I saw Karan waiting for me with puppy eyes and a board that said, 'Sorry.'

He got me.

That night was the first time he satisfied me in bed. Usually, our nights were spent with him demanding as I obeyed. It was also the first time he had spent a night at my house. It felt special, but synthetic. Later that night, I couldn't sleep. Karan was snoring away to glory.

I lit a cigarette and walked into my balcony at 3 a.m. and contemplated what life had in store for me. Last year, I had been lonely and undesirable, and now I was wanted and loved. But something was amiss. I smoked the cigarette till the last drag and commanded my mind to stop. A small cluster of sighs and some unshed tears clamoured within me. I fought to find some composure.

7

I felt a pair of eyes on me all the time. Deva was watching my every move, and after he memorized the move, he would make his footprints be felt around me. He had the strategy of a deer; he ensured that he followed me at every step. He had a reason too—we were together on a secret project, which he mistook to be a secret affair between us.

I didn't stop him, perhaps because he felt like a back-up option when Karan was unpredictable. I felt shallow for even having thoughts like these but survival tactics were natural for me in any situation. My brain was programmed to move from Plan A to B to C. Living with the times. That's what I called it!

I'd been trying to interpret Karan when he had no consistent identity or behaviour. Having no consistent behaviour means having no consistent relationship. But by now, Deva knew my moods and learned my likes; he had crawled his way into my life. He was like the leech that sticks on to you and goes unnoticed till it stings.

We had a site visit planned, and Deva had a plan at

hand. I totally avoided going in his car but he had somehow convinced Mr Rebello that we both would join him after lunch together.

Karan and I were rocky, but certainly steady with our feelings for each other. It was a phase in the relationship. We could stay away from each other and not long to be around each other all the time. Karan said that it was always the woman who liked to cling. I was indifferent and I did not portray any such desires. So we stayed away, but we were together. It worked for me. But Karan wanted me to remain dependent on him.

The conversation went such. 'Where are you going after lunch?'

'Work.'

After a long pause and hopefully a lot of contemplation he messaged back. 'Out of the office?'

He quickly added an afterthought: 'Take care. Maybe I can drive you.'

'No, I'll manage. See you!'

Then I sat down and pondered over my cold behaviour. Were these my insecurities? Or was it that I had naturally created a shield around me? I validated my behaviour to myself and moved on.

In any case, after my momentary annoyance with Karan in the morning had passed, I was looking forward to a bright day.

Deva was a gentleman. He opened the car door for me, and quickly ran back to his door to start the air conditioning in the car. A car is a symbol of success in India. If you have a car, you are suddenly seen as successful. However, this was

Deva's father's car. There was a mildew smell in the car, but it looked new, cleaned and washed to impress. Deva looked over at me, turning the radio on as he gave me a meek smile. He adjusted his car air blowers towards me and we were off.

After a few minutes of deafening silence, I spoke. 'Should I start using Google maps to find the fastest route?'

When you live in Mumbai, you are a slave to Google maps; even the auto drivers in the city have their own maps turned on. We were going to reach earlier than predicted—an unheard-of phenomenon in a normal scenario, but with Deva's overriding excitement it was possible. The Mumbai standard time was one of its kind; people who were approximately one hour late were pardoned without apologies.

As it is said, music connects everybody. We hummed old Bollywood songs of the eighties and created a bond. We smiled and enacted the moves to the songs; grooved at the most endearing tunes which we had grown up with. It was special. I felt happy in the true sense, the happiness a child feels. I felt it once again after eternity!

The guilt was killing me, but my heart was asking me to let go and be in the moment. I could see that the ride encouraged him; he had never dreamed that a girl would accompany him, and certainly not someone like me. It was a sweet dream.

My mind is manipulative, so I decided to get rid of the guilt. Hence I blurted it out. 'I'm seeing someone, just thought you should know!' I said it.

But his reply was unexpected. 'I wouldn't expect anything less from a gorgeous lady like you!'

This was a sharp gamble. I wanted to win. I wanted him to treat me with special care and affection, but I didn't want the guilt that came with it. Men usually fall for traps like these and stay hopeful, continuing to pursue the woman even after knowing they are taken. In turn, the girl continues to feel safe because, in her head, she's made it clear and isn't cheating. This game can be a double-edged sword for the man who is pursuing, but more often than not, men choose to play along.

And so, Deva opened the door when we reached the site. I smiled and maybe even blushed. Then I looked at him and saw how unattractive he was…but his heart was gold.

'Right here!' Mr Rebello pointed at the tall, modern, futuristic tower with glass walls, which were covering the rhombus shape of the tower. From an aerial view, it would look like a spaceship ready to take off. The tapering tip of the building made the structure a unique sight to the eyes. Each floor had vertical gardens and some had attached terrace offices. It was a dream work place for many, but for me, it only meant driving further; longer hours on the road with the brain-wrecking traffic.

Mr Rebello was gasping for breath as he turned to the stairway. 'The elevators have not started yet so we have to take the stairs.'

Deva looked over his shoulder and smirked at me. It was a hilarious sight. I couldn't help it and a slight laugh escaped me, as if I was lauding what Deva was implying.

Obviously, soon enough, the boss almost knelt to his knees and walked like a duck. Climbing six floors was a cakewalk for Deva. Even though he looked meek, he was actually a strong man.

Inside, the office space was exquisite—glass windows, top to bottom, and marbled engraved floors. The logo of the office was engraved on the reception floor. That was my brainchild. I had suggested it casually to Mr Rebello, he didn't react then but he had clearly taken the idea (and most probably the credit too).

While walking into the cabins, I saw that they looked smaller than the current ones.

'The cabins are smaller. But we don't have a choice, the layout is scattered.' Mr Rebello gave this non-explanation to no one in particular.

'Why don't we remove the cabins altogether? We could then accommodate everyone without paying the rent of the current space.' Deva spoke casually.

Mr Rebello's eyes sparkled, but he kept his calm. He was going to use this idea, I knew it! He would later make it his own.

Suddenly, we thought we saw a shadow. I walked towards it but didn't find anyone. Deva raised his eyebrows at me.

'I thought I saw someone, maybe a cat.'

We walked ahead. I was sure Deva was thinking the same things: why had the boss selected us? Maybe Deva was not that naive; he knew why we were chosen.

We walked around every corner of the office. I was starting to believe that I had watched too many murder mysteries of late and was hallucinating images and footsteps.

I was unaware of this at that time, but now I know

it was Karan. He was right behind us, following our car when I was with Deva, right behind me when I was walking up the stairs. Stalking and doubting my every move. He was right behind my back. He peeped over my messages. Ignorant about his tactics and his eye on me all the time, I had blindly believed him. I didn't know! How could I have known? 'Had he done this to every girl he had dated? Was he just jealous of Deva?'

But I didn't know then. He did this behind my back.

And I loved him as much as I could.

He was following every step I took. 'Was he a narcissist in the making? Or was he just a serial loser? Why would he be jealous of someone like Deva? Did he feel threatened when I didn't tell him where I was going? How long had he been following me? Was he going to harm me?'

His feet always whispered across the floor but he had the sort of stealth that only trained killers possess. And I was unaware about this entire thing as it happened behind my back!

The Meera fifteen years later would understand this, but the Meera back then, in that exact moment, couldn't even fathom this behaviour.

A text beeped: 'I love you and I'm sorry!' Karan had brought an instant smile back to my lips. I realized how puerile our fight had been, and I sent a kiss back.

Later, that night, we made passionate love; something that I had rarely experienced with him before. Traces of Abhi kept coming back to me while I was with Karan, but I nudged that thought aside. I felt more comfortable not thinking about who it was that I was having sex with and soon I transcend into sheer pleasure.

But at the back of my mind, I thought of Abhi. He stood there impassive, his arms folded, patiently waiting for me to leave. If I asked myself, whether the sexcapades with him had been worth it, his body language alone would have answered with a resounding no! And yet...

Karan rolled back on the bed immediately after and fell into a deep sleep. I found it hard to sleep next to someone. I'd always been alone and liked to be alone. But I didn't ask him to leave, primarily because I felt guilt that I had doubted him. He had done nothing but love me. I let him stay at my house again. It was the beginning of a journey I wanted to endure. He slept like a baby, sound and carefree; but not soundless, his snores could scare Kumbhkaran. I gasped and convinced myself, I'll survive!

I walked towards the balcony and saw Abhi sitting on the same chair he always sat on, smoking his lungs out. That's when I reckoned that Abhi wasn't lonely by force but by choice. I gave him a meek smile. He raised his eyebrows and made a mysterious gesture, almost like asking if I was okay.

Was I okay?

I wasn't sure yet!

I made myself a drink and came back to the balcony. I sipped on the whiskey and waited for the sunrise.

I woke up to a gentle kiss on my forehead.

'Why did you sleep on the balcony?' Karan asked. He was genuinely concerned.

'Because you snore too loudly,' I said and we both laughed.

He carried me to the room where I saw that he had made me a cup of hot masala tea. He was surely an angel, dropped here just for me. Though I was often sceptical, I had to thank god for looking out for me.

Mysteriously, my phone was locked. I was annoyed and shoved it inside the purse without a thought. While Karan left early for a shower, I was left behind with some time on my bed; his smell lingered on the bed sheet. All I needed was five minutes.

It was an odd day. While pulling my dupatta over my shoulders, I saw Abhi. He was dressed in his best formals: cotton pink and slim white-buttoned shirt with beige trousers. He peered through me, but I didn't flinch. I didn't have the energy to see him right now. *Not now!* I was clear enough in my head, as if it would stop me from thinking about him. This wasn't the time!

Wanting to rethink my actions, I decided that a walk through the beach was the only solution. Karan. Cause and effect. I was conducting myself erratically. I felt that love was madness. I shouted at myself—loud and clear as the wind blew on my face. It forced my tears to dry quicker than they could form. 'You always find ways to push away anyone who comes close to you.'

It may be the actions of a child who has been hurt. As a small girl, I was so desperate for refuge that I called a truce with every erring guy, with all the small snubs and cruelties that came with it. I had found living in my aunt's house a lot easier than at my own place that I now called home.

At the office, far through the glass corridors, a blurred

image of Saira passed by. She was just the person I was looking for. My sanity in insanity, she was my calm. And suddenly, she stood in front of me, making me think I was losing sense of time and space. But an instant smile ran over my lips, almost like she had the button to activate my smile. Her forehead wrinkled when she saw me, and then she let out a sigh. 'You might think you are a mystery, but in reality you are more transparent than a glass,' she said.

Smiling, I replied. 'It's just a bad morning.' Then we bolted to the recharge centre—the terrace.

The best thing about Saira was that she never judged me, and when she did, she said it aloud. Then the words were out there in the open, open for discussion.

It helped to get some fresh air. Deva was already at the terrace even though he didn't smoke. When he walked towards us, I blushed. I tried to keep myself in check, even though a little flirting never hurt. I was disillusioned. My mind was speaking a different language when compared to my heart.

Just then, I read a large caption on a billboard. I read the one message I had needed to hear. 'Only a monk can keep his mind, body, heart and soul aligned, so lower your expectations.'

Deva was standing right there, hitting it off with Saira. Until last month, no one had known this man had a tongue. Then, almost like he had heard my thoughts, he walked to me, smiled and said, 'Thank you.'

I tried to make a guess not knowing why he was grateful.

He continued, 'No one would notice me, if it wasn't for you,' he said.

Secretly, I know that my colleagues now noticed me because there was a buzz about who the girl with Karan was. I owed Karan for it, but I had never told him. I liked not having to say anything. It was addictive, even though I knew my gratitude too needed to be expressed. I believed that it had been said without being said. It was easier to be silent than to acknowledge my emotions.

Karan walked into the terrace. It was his time for a smoke. I didn't think my sane mind could handle this group of people together. I asked Saira for a cigarette, and Karan came up and immediately pulled one out from his packet. I grabbed at it rather quickly.

I was certain that I needed to leave, but I froze. I stood right there.

Saira gave me an exasperated look. She had recently sent me a message. 'Your mind is your worst enemy.' It was true! She had magical powers and could see through me.

Deva and Karan, oblivious to the explosions in my head, were both looking at me. Karan, out of habit, put his hand around my waist. This was nothing new but I saw Deva twitch.

Karan, being his abrasive self, asked him, 'What are you working on lately?' He paused and continued. 'Rather, which department are you from?' Karan had a knack. He could make people feel tiny.

If only I had accepted it—things would have been different for Karan. He would have another person feeling shaky in front of him.

Weeks passed. Karan spent his nights with me. It became the new normal. I grew habituated to his snoring and to him being around all the time. He now took over the space I had created for myself. But he was cooking for me and was often able to satisfy my expectations. He wasn't meeting my needs fully, but he was trying; and I was meeting him in between the road. In today's world we call it compromise.

The weird thing was that he now rarely invited me to his place, and if I ever asked, he played the bachelor card. 'Hey I am a man, my house is dirty. You will not like it there.'

'I would like to clean up your house sometime,' I would retaliate, but that *some* time never came.

He made excuses every week to such an extent that I started doubting the existence of his house altogether. Foolish as I was in love, but my natural instinct of doubt lingered. It left me confused. He continued to stay a mystery.

But he would walk towards me and I felt better.

Tonight he was in his pajamas. We shared a few shots of vodka and soon, I relaxed in his presence. I told myself to be positive, which was easier. As he slipped his hand into my blouse, I decided to take pleasure in what I have. I ignored the thoughts crawling into my brain and just flowed with his moves. I was learning to love him and teaching him to love me as well.

As I sat on the edge of the bed, smoking, naked, I did feel connected to him.

But the more I stayed with Karan, the more pessimistic I was becoming. I had to force myself to be optimistic. This was a deep abyss with no exit.

Putting on my clothes, I wandered into the balcony. There was something about the balcony that called out for me. The place felt secure and I could also see the world below while nestled inside my cocoon. Stretching towards the side, I clandestinely looked up, and I saw Abhi smiling at me, about to say something.

Karan walked up behind me. Abhi was taken aback and retreated to his room.

The whole situation wasn't odd at all, not until Karan authoritatively asked, 'Who was he?'

I don't know if I wanted to get used to someone questioning me. Especially not if someone did it with authority, as if they owned me. It ticked the side of me that can get aggressive. I immediately tried to calm my nerves and closed my eyes. I replied as calmly as I could. 'How does it matter to you?'

'Why would an unknown man try to talk to you in the middle of the night? And go away at the sight of your boyfriend walking in?' This time his pitch was higher.

I looked at him and replied. 'Maybe because you don't seem like you have a pleasant personality.' I knew I had poked the lion, but I was a lioness.

He pulled me back by my arm and pushed me back on the bed. My head hurt the headboard with a sound. He ignored it in his rage.

'Have you slept with him?' he yelled while charging towards me.

My head hurt from the collision, but I was petrified. I didn't know what he would do next. He rushed towards me, reached out as if to strangle me and then astonishingly, slowly fell behind, half hanging from the bed. He lay there for a good five minutes or more. I was confused, and guessed it must be a concussion by falling so hard on the bed and he must have hurt his head or he was too drunk, or maybe he just fainted due to some injury he got while charging towards me. But in all he was unconscious.

I was horrified. I couldn't move so I stayed there. I probably had a concussion too.

Was he dead?

I slid a little and slipped out of the bed. I made a mental note of the kitchen weapons I could use when he woke up. He didn't move the entire night. I sat there, shivering with fear that he might wake up. I wanted to leave but I was frozen throughout the night. I couldn't sleep a wink until I saw him shift with the first rays of the sun.

I thought quickly. 'Should I move away? Should I act like I'm asleep? Should I confront him? Or should I hit him so hard that he falls again and is unconscious? Did this happen… or was this my imagination? Was I drugged? Was I drunk? Was he also drunk?' These questions formed a queue in my head like a domino. I wasn't willing to believe this was reality.

He rolled on his side and moaned with pain. He held his head where it seemed to have hurt him and then he opened his eyes. I was so scared that I gritted my teeth and closed my eyes. I dread seeing the horror.

I had prayed hard all night, run through all the shlokas I'd learned as a kid.

And boom, he had woken up!

He scanned the place and as he saw me, his eyes turned into slits. Seeing me sitting, he glared.

I rushed through my worries.

'Was he looking at me?
Did he go back to sleep like that?
Would he hurt me again?
Did he notice the blood stains on the bed?
Was he trying to recollect the events of last night?
What was he thinking?
Will he attack me again?'

I stayed numb, waiting for his reaction, looking for any traces of the extreme emotions that he had displayed. Something that assured me that I'd be alive. His bloodshot gaze towards me felt like an icicle piercing through my chest. My throat went dry and the lump in my heart was throbbing painfully.

His face calmed and his lips shaped into a curve that looked like a smile. My heart felt a single smashing wave of happiness. He stood up and moved a few steps, and then, he walked to the kitchen.

He turned back to me and asked, 'Do you want coffee, darling?'

He rubbed at his head and felt a bump. 'Looks like I slept on the wrong side of the bed.'

He was unmoved. 'How can it be that he has no recollection of the previous night? Can it be? How can it be? He was on the verge of strangling me? Yet, he has no recollection of the previous night! He doesn't remember anything...or maybe, he does, and is simply playing coy, trying not to look aggressive. To save face, he has decided that he won't be talking about it, like it hasn't occurred at all.

Maybe if I told him about it he would say I am psychotic.' It jolted me and made me wonder if it had really happened.

Not wanting to remind him of the previous night, I quickly replied. 'Yes.' Then I ran to gather my clothes and rushed to the shower.

In the past, he has often left the coffee on the kitchen top and gone back home to shower. But I didn't even know where he really stayed. Of course, he had invited me to his place, but was that even his real house. Last night, made me think that he was crossing the line between normal and psychopathic behaviour.

Turbulent thoughts crossed my head, and that's when I heard him say, 'I'll go home and shower, see you at work!'

Relieved, I sat on the floor of the bathroom and sobbed softly.

The events of the previous night played in front of me. Karan had tried to assault and strangle me, he hit my head, he had shattered my body, and then he had fallen, as if dead, on the bed unconscious.

Despite the physical and emotional trauma, I had found some strength. I had survived by hiding the whole night and praying. Then he had left as if nothing had happened.

I covered my mouth tightly with my hands. Tears rolled down my bloodshot eyes. I was breathing heavily, gasping for breath.

That day, I felt fear like never before, the fear of death.

8

I walked into the sun like I had never been burnt. I felt the light on my face and soaked the golden rays into my mind, body and soul. It felt like a new day and a new beginning. The whole month had been a roller coaster ride with the new office plans and more time with Deva.

My apartment building had a beautiful garden. I noticed today that the entire garden had been razed and now an unsightly, high, cemented platform stood in its place. I mourned all the plants that had adorned the place. My eyes went to where the rows of the marigold had been. A few withered stems of marigold oddly fought the slaughter and grew at the edge of the platform. They were scarcely alive. I looked up at Abhi's balcony. Now the balcony was empty. I suddenly felt an agonizing thought capturing my mind, but I did not exactly know what it was.

Half a day after my worst nightmare, I walked into the cafeteria and saw Deva and Karan sipping on the seasonal coconut water, waiting for their food to heat. They were not conversing with each other but were probably waiting for me. Now I saw the stark difference between the two of them. It perturbed me and I pondered over the mess that I had created by bringing two opposite worlds together. All I could do was turn my eyes away and try to walk away when Saira grabbed me by my waist.

It made me skip a beat. I didn't want to be touched. It scared me. Last night, the horrifying incident had scarred me, probably forever. It might take a lifetime to be held by someone again.

I grabbed her hand and rushed her to the elevator. I had to tell her what happened to me. We took the ground floor; we stood in silence for a while. She knew I was horrified, she could see it in my eyes.

I told her every detail, every moment of terror that I had spent in the night. About my fear of death. I reiterated it to her, breath by breath, act by act. While spelling it out in words, it felt more intense and violent than it had sounded in my head. I was shell shocked and was dreading whatever was in store.

Saira chose her words carefully and said, 'And you said that in the morning, he forgot?'

Uncertain about my own response, I said, 'Yes. Maybe... I don't know.' And finally. 'But he didn't discuss it!'

Laying out the sentence, word by word, for me to ponder over, and for her to judiciously assess the situation, Saira was once again cautious as she asked, 'Has he behaved similarly before?'

The question hit me hard. It made me comb through my memory. I couldn't think of any instance of him being violent. No, but he surely was aggressive. While Saira was recouping from the horror of the situation, I wracked my brain. He was always angry about small things; small things would enrage him.

'Now that you're asking his rage levels are higher than that of a normal person. He has a rakish manner, even though he is very attractive,' Saira said. She paused and sipped on her coffee. 'He also likes to show off his masculine overpowering side more than usual. He is a bit extreme, but in a latent way.'

After a lot of pondering, while Saira did not say a word, I thought some more. Then, allowing myself to open up, I said, *'I am probably overthinking.'*

A part of me didn't want this to be true and I believed in myself. I wanted to think that I was capable of selecting a good partner who was kind and compassionate, not a psychopath who would attack me in the dark of the night. My mind was convincing me to not think, and it was working. I was convinced. This event had been a one-time occurrence in the wake of intoxication.

I shut up, and so did Saira.

Saira and I decided to take a short walk to the shore after which we headed back towards the office.

It was an odd feeling to walk back into the familiar lobby, there was something different. There was a new feeling in my throat, a lump so big it was hard to swallow. I was catching the flu, I thought. My body's defenses were down and this was an indication that I should try some soothing techniques.

Work was slow, so I banked on the first change to catch a meditation class. Human beings are selfish. Only when they face hardship do they pray to god, only when they feel pain do they protest, only when they face adversity do they whine about life being unfair. When roses are blooming and life is fragrant, no one is grateful. We are a thankless species, and we only think about the divine or all-encompassing power when life is rocky.

Meditation, by the way, has nothing to do with god, but it is the closest you can get to your soul to come back to life. It is a place where nothing is beautiful and nothing is ugly. It is the place of nothingness, which you can reach only if you believe in such a place. But even this explanation belittles the magnificence of the process. Many people believe that meditation is connected to a religion or to a particular god. But for me it's just a place of infinity!

Changing into my yoga pants, something struck me. I didn't want to think about it, but it was true. I had gained a few pounds. Considering the stress I was undergoing, I would have expected that I was losing weight. But when something goes wrong, many other things go wrong too.

I sat in padmasana, and I tried to not think of Karan. It was the hardest part. When other people discussed how they couldn't stop thinking, it always made me wonder: 'How can one not concentrate?'

Here I was, judged by my own judgment.

I tried hard again and on the forty-first minute a miracle occurred. The fog around my head cleared and I could clearly see the deep blue ocean and the happy dolphins. The mammals did not smile or frown; they were simply content with what they had and seemed full of gratitude and serenity. I got lost in their expressions, and I wondered what they were feeling every time they gracefully came out of the water. Every slender movement they made showed no creases on their face. One particular baby dolphin had a different expression. It seemed to chuckle, to express bewilderment, anticipation and admiration. The baby dolphin then looked at me and gazed into my eyes. The gaze was clear and hopeful.

I was deep in my thoughts. The chanting music had taken me to a place in my subconscious, a place that wasn't accessible easily.

After this, with renewed energies, I walked towards home, beaming with optimism.

Karan was out with his friends. It made me wonder who his friends were, but I dared not ask him.

A message beeped.

'Coffee?'

It was Deva.

I quickly replied, leaning towards sounding desperate.

'Sure. CCD? Near my house?'

His reply was quicker than mine had been. 'Be there in thirty.'

The CCD near my house was my second home. I knew the staff there at every shift. They knew my usual and they treated me well. It was my comfort zone—my khichdi. Funnily enough, I had never been there with Karan. After all, we had jumped into sex and the courtship period had been rather short.

Sometimes I wonder, why your mind is your slave. It makes you believe what you want to believe. When you want to believe in someone, it clings to the happy memories and replays the times when you felt special. And when you want to lose faith in someone, it reminds you of the same times and replays the negative feelings you had during that time. As it is said: where there is black, there is also white. It's the balance that keeps us sane. We can always fool ourselves into believing in what's not in front of us. Our mind is our own homegrown palace of illusions. Water it when you want and fertilise it as you need!

Interrupting my thoughts, Deva entered the cafe in a pearl white shirt and blue jeans. It could pass as a formal dinner shirt. He made heads turn but not in admiration. Despite his being almost thirty, there was something simple and unrestricted about him. He was sharp and eager. But he always seemed to be in a state of repose and calm. The only part about him that was untamed and alive were his eyes, and they burned now with a question I could not identify. But the best thing about him was stability, he was stable.

I let out a smirk but then regained my composure swiftly.

Deva came and sat next to me. He seemed surprised, as if he couldn't believe that I really was there, waiting for him. For a few moments, my mind went just foggy seeing him in white and blue denim. I couldn't see what was around me. The daunting presence of other people faded from my sight. All my senses probably concentrated on just one truth. Deva.

Seeing me sitting in my hoodie and shorts should have made him feel overdressed, but he showed no hint of any embarrassment. The beauty of people like him is that their naivete is magnetising. He cordially ordered his coffee and also got one for me, then he brought along some pastries to go with it and sat opposite me.

Everything he did was different from what Karan would have done. But I checked my thoughts. I knew they were corrupted right now and partial towards Deva. We enjoyed our coffee and chatted about nothing in particular. No big agendas, no forced conversation, no awkward silence. We were just two friends catching up. We laughed out loud when he mimicked Rebello. Bystanders were equally amused when he aped Rebello's walk. It was a light evening, a much-needed respite from the madness I was experiencing of late.

Weeks passed, and nightmares had become my best friend. I was still shattered about what had happened. A month after that unfortunate night, Karan said he wanted to come over to spend the night.

But the incident had occurred only a month ago! So, I programmed my mind to think differently about it. 'It wasn't what it looked like. Maybe he was coming to hug me, as opposed to what I thought he was doing—that he was trying to attack me. Maybe he intended to throw me sexily on the bed and not push me.' I had a lot of doubts and questioned myself daily.

Once, I told Saira about these questions and she was furious. She believed Karan was evil and wanted me to accept that, but in the past one month he had only been kind and generous and affectionate with me. My mind was fine-tuning the positives of Karan, lately.

I wanted to forget about it, but Saira kept reminding me. Human beings are animals of habit. Once a human is habituated to someone, it's hard to let go. On the other hand, if a human has never known of the existence of something, it does not cause any discomfort.

If you haven't tasted blood, you don't know how it tastes. But once you have, it is impossible to let go. As a slave to my body, I gave in to my temptations.

Abhi was like a ghost now. He always appeared at my most vulnerable moments. One night, I woke up trembling, images of Karan strangling me had visited me in my nightmares. This recurring nightmare had not left me and now sleeping was a curse.

Abhi looked at me on the balcony with longing eyes, but I resisted him. We exchanged a few glances and a few texts, but I retreated to my bed. Laying there, on the bed, I stared at the ceiling fan. It was moving slowly, but it still seemed faster than me.

I slept.

Over the next few days, I was busy with the work on the new project with Deva and Rebello. It helped me find respite from the darkness. I had a few chats with Karan but we hadn't spent time together. Every time he suggested meeting, I'd give him a valid excuse about work. Saira was my shield. As soon as Karan tried talking to me, Saira would magically appear from somewhere. She cared for me. I saw that, but more than that, she hated Karan. They were antagonistic to each other.

With the new office space coming up, I was also spending more time at the new location. This made Karan skittish. There were times when his messages would be rash, and then he would immediately delete it. His impulses would bring out the worst in him, but he would correct his actions immediately. I could see that he was struggling.

The office space looked beautiful. The lavish white marble shone, as did the exquisite artwork at the entrance. There, Deva and I were alone. I cherish that time with him. He wasn't worldly or smart, but he had a heart of gold. Every day he came to pick me and he drove me when we had to go to the new location. Often, we would sit on the floor and drink our tea, looking over the ocean with the golden lining on the waves. Some days, we wouldn't have time to even look at each other, since we had a lot to accomplish. But there was synchronicity in our teamwork. We were great together. We continued our work and many nights we would go to a small roadside place for tea and dinner. It was a ritual that we had created for a few weeks. Then he would drop me home. It was blissful bond. It was precious!

I knew, deep inside, that he would do anything to be a part of my life. I knew he would treat me like a queen. The way every woman wants to be treated as. But even though I wasn't with Karan the way I used to be, I thought I would be cheating. Karan was already out to make me feel guilty.

The more I looked, the more I saw a host of changes in him. I didn't feel safe enough to be with him behind the closed doors of my apartment. Contemplating how my life had altered within a few months made me gasp.

I was enjoying some coconut water with Deva while listening to some old songs by Kishore, and Karan asked me, probably for the hundredth time, to meet him. I thought, not once had he apologized. He had sent me flowers, gifts and many other messages. But there had been no apology.

I believe that one act can change your life. On the other hand, I'm also an optimist and believe that even the darkest days have a ray of light. And I try and try till I reach the sun. That was always me, even though I lose myself sometimes. I'm mostly driven by optimism, sometimes blatantly foolish optimism too. At times I had moved past the worst with strength. But now, with Karan, I didn't want to manipulate myself into believing something that was not true. I wanted to think with my head. I wanted this to be an organic return and not influenced.

I enjoyed our peaceful time in the new office, especially since Rebello was always missing. It was usually the two of us and a handful of people from the office. We did things from scratch: infrastructure, IT, telecommunication. I was on a high at work. I loved organising the place and it was a good distraction.

Our team of six ate together and worked together. We worked long hours to complete our own tasks. We wanted to have everything ready before our deadline. Since Rebello had put me in charge of the project, it was a huge responsibility. I wanted it to be perfect and wanted the transition to be effortless.

The work felt like a big party, but with a lot to do. However, there was no stress and it all felt smooth, like a river flowing.

Since the six of us had been working together, we understood each other and were in full harmony. It felt like this would be one of the most enriching experiences at work for me. I had never felt so satisfied and motivated. Rebello's incapability or fear of commitment had given me the chance of my lifetime.

We had almost completed all the work and now the staff would have to be shifted from one department to another the next week. However, before that we wanted to celebrate our victory! The amount of work done in such a short time was appreciated, even by the overseas office. We all got an appreciation email from the head in America. We were all overjoyed.

And, Deva and I seemed to have shared intimate moments with each other in this period without even touching each other. We had forged a bond that was unspoken. What we had was now unbreakable.

Soon, I resumed my daily work in silence.

All the chatter had deserted me. What I had with Deva kept me going. I recognized we had a sense of warmth. So many of my beautiful moments, moments of living and normalcy, had come to be associated with him. It flowed like peace through me.

At the desk, I looked to find Deva scrutinising me.

Perhaps all my feelings towards Deva were gratuitous, even unsanctioned when I still had Karan in my mind. I battled my guilt.

Deva too understood that we could not be together. But he also understood that right now there wasn't any other relationship that mattered to me more than being with him. It was true friendship.

9

Days after settling into the new office, I dreaded that I had no excuses left to not meet Karan. Yes, finally I was accepting the fear that incident had inflicted upon me, but Karan had been kind and understanding.

'One of the reasons he is kind is because he feels guilty,' said Saira. Saira still hated him, but she liked Deva.

She had sworn to not let Karan around me. So Karan was following Saira, waiting, so that when she slipped away he could catch a chat with me. It felt like I was in high school—managing relationships.

In any case, talking about the spending habits of a MNC and the thing about working for a multinational is that no one understands budgets. It is a party all the time. No one cares because it's no one's money, so everyone finds innovative ways to spend the funds coming from a foreign account using a fictitious name or a con call every month. Here we throw figures and jargon, confusing and derailing the real reason and concern at hand for the next meet or the annual meet.

We unanimously decided to come up with a new way

to spend the money we had already spent. We created a need to celebrate and threw a party. This party was to be my responsibility, and so I religiously asked Rebello what the limit would be on the expenditure on this so-called opening party for our staff and their family. Rebello forgot to ask how much we should be spending, and then he decided on a sum himself. He gave me a random amount in hand, which seemed very generous to me and told me to organise it.

Deva and I, aware of the company's debts, decided to have a low-key party. But this too seemed quite expensive.

Deva said, 'I really don't feel like we are being loyal to our employer by doing these unnecessary expenditures.'

Rebello, on the other hand, said, 'Let's get a live band to help the mood.'

I wanted to ask about the mood but refrained. I know what would come next. What happens to companies like ours is that because of inconsistent expenditure and incomes not rounded off, eventually there are mass terminations or salary reductions. In turn, it always comes back to the employees, but not everyone saw this. Ignorance isn't bliss, it's a curse in all its forms. When the employee feels that he is a partner in the company, he will be equally liable for the performance of the company. He will care for his own well-being and that of the company, but this was very bookish wisdom for Rebello. He was short-sighted.

So we did what we were told. We found a band. And then we found caterers. And then we found some party planners who did the same job. Opulence at someone else's cost is always a pleasure, but Deva and I frowned upon it. Rebello was on a roller coaster high. He had been showered with praise by the overseas head office. They were stumped by how fast the transition had been, and it had saved them a year's rent. They had called in the team for a video call to appreciate our efforts, but Rebello had said that the team was too busy working and hence could not attend. But he attended that meeting and took the credit for all our hard work.

We had known from the beginning; he had selected us as a team to make sure no one shone brighter than him at the time of completion.

However, the appreciation email we had already received from the head office, in recognition of our efforts, was enough for us to feel special. We were creatures of habit. All we did was feel good about the email. None of us even replied with a thank you. We should have been taught to respond to appreciation as kids, maybe in school. What was the point of learning calculus when we weren't taught to express ourselves? Our education system, even though it is exhaustive, didn't teach us to be confident and respect ourselves. And now, everything we need to know is just a fingertip away, and we still know nothing. We should have been taught life skills, but instead, we learned to choose safe paths. We were told to always listen to elders, which was the first mistake. We were told so many things, and these things have been slow killers when it came to our progress.

Deva dropped me back home before the party so I could change. I had already known that Karan wouldn't come with me. He didn't want anyone in the office to know about us dating, but he never flinched before callously holding me by the waist within office premises. It had hurt earlier, but now it comforted me, I had an escape route.

I wanted this celebration to also celebrate my achievement, so I wanted to party hard. After all, we had to celebrate the new office and my friendship with Deva. But I was also scared of being around Karan after such a long time. I had been talking to him, in bits and pieces. Saira, my shield, had always been trying to protect me from him. She had been my bedrock, besides Deva. Deva, however, was a product of timing. Somehow, he had landed up next to me at the right time and at the right place for the right job.

I was in a celebratory mood and wanted to dress for the occasion. I pulled out my best outfit—a modest but classic look. A dreamy silk, pink halter-top paired with beige georgette loose trousers. I wore my high heels and put on nude makeup. I paired all this with oversized hoop earrings. Glancing into the mirror, I reckoned I could most definitely turn a few heads. I looked lustrous. I had been dipped in success.

I carefully walked down the building, trying to not slip on the muddy water. The rainwater was splashing around like falling stars. Some drops landed like a burst of happiness right on my cheeks. The soft caress of the rain felt like dew drops, like healing.

The entire burden I was holding on to slowly passed. I could feel my shoulders relax—it was if I was released, unchained. I made a decision to take a risk. I decided to give Karan another chance.

As I walked down the stairs, I felt renewed, like a newborn

baby. I had a new life. I never thought I'd get past the incident, but his persistence had got me to review my stern decision. Of course, at the back of my mind, I knew that I needed him as much as he needed me. Life can surprise you, someone who didn't need anyone just a year before now needed someone beside her. 'Am I making a mistake?' My heart was pounding.

Deva was there to pick me up, and it made me wonder if he just changed in his car and returned. There is something about Deva. Whenever I see him, my nerves calm down. Part of the reason I wanted to sort things out with Karan was Deva.

Hadn't I already fallen for Karan, Deva would have been my best chance to find real love...

I didn't understand why I thought that I would fall for Deva. He was shy. He didn't seem to have a lot of future prospects. He was someone who sat in the corner and didn't raise a voice, but also someone who was compassionate and in tune with me, like no one had ever been. Deep down I knew the reason, because he loved me, his eyes spoke. But then I convinced myself I was in tune with Saira too, and that did not mean I should go out with her.

My head was spinning.

I saw Deva standing in front of the building with an open umbrella in his hand. He looked dashing in his black crisp linen shirt and black trousers. He had even put on cufflinks, they seemed quite out of the ordinary. His jaw dropped at the sight of me.

He looked at me with a yearning hope. I saw that he was crazy about me. What I saw in his eyes, I had never seen in Karan's. Karan's eyes had lust, Deva's eyes felt like warm heat on a cold night; but my heart still wanted Karan. Something about the devil was more attractive.

Deva was walking towards me. He couldn't take his eyes off me. I felt like a teenager with butterflies in my stomach. I felt beautiful with him. He opened the door for me.

Throughout the car ride, it was quiet but his company felt gratifying. I was grateful to have a friend like him.

We reached the venue and found that it was a madhouse. The place hadn't been set up and the caterers had not yet shown up. And the decorators—the little work they had to do had still not been completed. It was utter chaos and I saw my colleagues almost breaking down. What we did not have to face while opening the office, we were facing at the party. We weren't used to hosting parties and it was evident. There was an hour before the party and we had got it all wrong.

I was running from pillar to post. I had put my dainty heels away and walked barefoot. I lifted tables and chairs to ensure the setup was ready on time. Deva was continuously on a call with the band as they had magically disappeared. They had initially bombarded us with calls and messages, but since the afternoon, our messages had gone unanswered. I could see Deva nervous as a mouse. He didn't work well where he had no control.

I just squeezed his shoulder and told him. 'Don't worry, we will find them. They are probably stuck in traffic.'

I lied, but I had to keep him sane.

As a treat for sore eyes, we saw that the caterers had just arrived and the set-up was coming together.

I grunted under my breath. 'Why are there only three people decorating?'

Those three decorators looked ashamed. They said that their boss had deployed most of the others for some larger event. It wasn't fair on me to rant at them for the mismanagement, plus it wouldn't get the work done. So I lent my hand to finish the job on time.

The time was ticking away and I could see some of our staff walking in. Saira was one of the first few to come and when she saw the place in that state, she started helping too.

And then, the band arrived. I had never before felt so relieved to see a group of smelly men with instruments in my whole life. I just didn't want the event to fall apart after all the hard work that had gone into the actual opening of the office.

Finally, the place was set and everything was in order. Just in time. As everyone came in, they wouldn't have fathomed the chaos we were in just ten minutes ago. But that's what event management is all about—making it look pretty when it matters.

In my haste, I had almost forgotten to care about how I looked. I had tied my hair in a bun and spoiled the blow dry. I was sweating. I was confident that I looked like a disaster. I tried to catch a glimpse of myself in the glass reflection, but to my dismay, I couldn't see the person I'd looked a while ago. This whole ordeal had killed my zeal to look good and slay the party. At this point, I just wanted it to be over.

As excited as he could be, Deva walked past me and whispered a sweet murmur into my ear. 'You still look gorgeous.' This was the first time that he had said something that made me shiver. It brightened my face up. I even blushed a little.

All's well that ends well.

As I stepped back, I looked at the classic decor, the fresh flowers and some glow lights. The effort had been worthwhile. And we were ready before time, before most people arrived. When Rebello walked in, he was delighted. I saw a little twinkle in his eyes.

Saira had come in a simple red dress and she just looked stunning. Rushing towards me she exclaimed, 'Good job, girl!'

Finally, Karan came in. He looked handsome, to say the least. As soon as he entered the hall, he walked towards me. He greeted me in a gentlemanly fashion and said I looked beautiful. The passion in him was missing. He could be cold and distant while saying the right things sometimes. It was as if he had an invisible and impenetrable wall around him.

But it was reaffirming to not feel unsafe around him again.

But then he did something unimaginable. We had a deal to keep our relationship private because Karan wanted that. Perhaps regretting his decision and in trying to make it right, he held my hand and walked with me. He was indirectly declaring me as his own. It gave me chills. I was instantly frozen. Everyone stared at us. I was a nobody in the office and he was the most sought-after bachelor. There were rumours about our affair, but this act sealed the deal and confirmed the rumours.

It surprised me! The murmurs were growing louder than the music. And all eyes were glued to my hand, which Karan was holding.

It felt good. It gave me an acceptance I never knew I yearned for. Karan was unmoved, his expressions didn't seem tense nor was his heart racing. He was as calm as he would be while walking in the park.

He was an unpredictable man, I thought. This action was, however, also making me uncomfortable. It made me question my own understanding of myself. But I wanted to enjoy the moment. For the first time in my life, a man had accepted me openly and wanted me openly. The feelings were mutual and my heart was yearning for him.

I tried pushing the memory of that dark night on the back of my brain, but it kept jutting its ugly head out.

I wouldn't let that stop me today. I knew my mind was stronger than my fears. Was I being foolish? Maybe, I was.

One person I couldn't ignore was Saira. She was furious on seeing me and Karan together, and she became almost violent when Karan held my hand. Saira charged towards me, fuming with rage and heartfelt consideration for my well-being. She held both these opposing feelings perfectly at the same time. I knew that there were only two people in the room whom I could vouch for, and say that they wanted me to be happy. They were Saira and Deva. But I avoided eye contact with Saira, like a little child who had done something wrong. She was the mother in the relationship, and I was the rebellious daughter.

Stomping her way towards me, she pinched my arm hard enough to pull the skin off.

'Have you lost your mind, why are you prancing around with this violent monster?' she paused exasperatedly and continued. 'Let me refresh your memory for you. He tried to physically hurt you!'

Saira could be so embarrassing. She could go to the extent of offending someone. I knew her well so I let it slide. She had my best interests in mind. I feared her as well since she had the aura of an authoritarian mother. Once in a meeting, she had even scolded the boss because he didn't follow the protocol. Despite her authoritarian attitude, she was respected for her advice. She squeezed my hand hard enough for me to let out a cry. She was furious, and in a bizarre manner, I wondered how gloriously I managed to bring out the violence in people. I gave out a chuckle.

The night turned out to be legendary for its opulence and indulgence. The party was obscenely grand. The guests marvelled at the interiors, the live band, the sumptuous food and most importantly, the unlimited liquor that we had generously supplied.

Karan was talking to some colleagues near the bar. After downing a few glasses of wine, I wished to hold Karan's hand again. This time I would be the one initiating it.

But images of him pushing me kept flashing in front of my eyes. At the beginning of the evening, he had seemed sober and desirable. But when the band took over, and as I counted his drinks and the amount of food he had consumed, it made me wonder if he was a Goliath. Men do have a huge appetite, but Karan's was always growing. And the way he ate, it was almost like an animal. He would slay as a poster boy for the sins of gluttony. My mental image of holding his hand shattered into pieces as I watched him jabbing his teeth into the roasted chicken like it was the last thing to eat on earth. I imagined horrifying scenes of him eating a live bird.

After dinner, everyone got to the dance floor. Most people were trying out their best moves and I was tipsy enough to behave like a drunk, grooving to the dance moves of my youth. Everyone was having a good time and dancing to the music. The quieter ones from the finance department rocked the dance floor the hardest and it was least expected. They surprised many young recruits.

Opposites attract, just like Karan and me. Because he was so different from me, I became suspicious about trusting him. The fear of the unknown was stopping me from getting my potential life partner. My own limitation was stopping me.

Right then, Saira dragged me away from the dance floor and warned again. 'Your mind is playing games with you. Telling you the false things to please your heart. Beware!'

I listened to her pleading and wanted her assurances because she was all I had. I didn't want to upset her. I needed her support. Love brings one closer to others. It softens you and I needed Saira's go ahead to try to love Karan.

'Had I just thought of it as love?'

I gave Saira a perplexed look when I realized my thoughts. Revealing this new information to her would be a mistake, a grave one. Instead I made puppy dog eyes and asked for her approval.

She dragged me towards the bar and gave me shots of vodka. After two shots, she nodded. It felt like her approval would wash away my doubts about Karan and I wanted it. After ordering one more shot with Saira, I twiddled towards

Karan. As this was an office party and I knew how much he hated public displays of affection, I stood out, trying to look calm and composed. He walked towards me standing alone. I was inviting him and he knew it. He stood right next to me and held my hand. The warmth of his hand replaced the lack of warmth in his aura. We stood there watching everyone dance. Not once did we look at each other. It felt like we were on a mission. Slowly, his hand moved towards my waist and he held me tighter like he owned me. I tried hard to remember the employee-dating policies. In that drunken state, I couldn't remember any.

He asked me politely, 'Shall we leave?' Just like a puppet, I nodded and followed right behind him.

We didn't speak much inside the taxi while he told the driver my address. I didn't protest, so that was my indirect acceptance. It helped that I was sloshed. I couldn't remember the past incident. It was wiped away as he helped me walk to my house. It felt like he had suddenly hypnotised me!

I had sworn to myself a month back that I would never be alone with him again, and now here I was, standing half naked in front of him in my own house of my own will. I always thought that I was strong and I wouldn't let anyone take advantage of me, that I would not have even an ounce of doubt in my partner. And here I was, surrendering to a man who had behaved like a psycho-killer.

I realized I was human and craved love. I was strong before when there were no stakes or takers. Now that I had a choice, I would risk myself.

Again, I let the alcohol take the blame for my decision.

10

He picked me up and put me on the bed. Then he jumped into the bed and we made love. He was tender and loving. Like always, he had very specific moves and he followed the rhythm.

He was never adventurous in bed, but today was different. He didn't stop; he kept going on.

It made me want him more and fired up my desires.

The alcohol blurred my vision and the dark made it harder to see. I kept squinting because it was dark in the room and the moon wore a crescent shape that night. Every time he leaned to kiss me, it was with increased vigour. And I responded with the same passion. Slowly it took on an ugly sight. If someone were watching it would look like we wanted to rip the skin off of the other, rip them apart to make the other a part of us.

There was intensity in his actions and he grabbed me towards him with force. He pulled me and I liked it. He used force while holding and caressing me; he pulled my hair at the back of my head and bit me on the neck. A part of me was humiliated in a way, but I liked it. The intoxication was making it easier to accept this as a form of sex and it looked like I consented to it.

He then pulled my hand behind me and whispered.

'Don't move.'

He nibbled on me and kissed me where he had nibbled. It was a rare kind of movement. Extremely pleasurable but unquestionably questionable.

When I woke up, my body was sore and there were bite marks everywhere, all over my body. And when I saw him sleeping, he had a few too. I was taken aback. This was when I stopped myself from thinking about it. I didn't want to give it too much of my time. I calmly told myself, 'It was an unfathomably pleasurable night!'

My takeaways from that night were that he initiated sex which was driven by physical force, driven by passion and driven by his canine desire. But the most important thing to note here was that I didn't protest. I didn't feel the same humiliation after some time, and I played along with the beat of the night. I had also started wanting what he had wanted and we were unified in our desire. It had started as one man's desire and had ended in a couple's wish to explore and innovate. It was very similar to what you see in movies or read in books. It felt like he had just gotten this scene out of a fantasy novel and tried to play it out. He seemed so confident in what he was doing and how he had done it. He was a different person in bed, not the same composed person I knew. At best, he could be defined as having a split personality in bed.

I had not seen that side of his personality before, and I never imagined it would be like that. The bruises on my body were obvious and needed tending, so I applied a balm on the red portions. While selecting clothes for the day, I picked a turtleneck full-sleeve top that hid the bite marks properly. Luckily, it was cool during the day and this way, I would avoid an interrogation from Saira. My pseudo-mother still didn't approve of my boyfriend. But it felt good to have someone to look after you, care for you.

Sleeping in wasn't an option. My mind was crowded. I went for a run to clear my head. After many days I was awake at dawn and I took the chance. Running in the early morning and seeing the sunrise gives me a different high. And I wanted that. The high that nature can give you is not comparable to any other high.

I started on a slower pace but after running the events of the last few months again inside my head, it made me anxious and I quickened. I went through the ups and downs again and again. I went back to how it was before Karan. Life was pleasant but predictable. Now it is exciting and dangerous. I saw my thoughts waver towards the negatives, so I naturally turned to music and put on my headphones. I wanted to reminisce the night and also enjoy my run, and that plan would be ruined if I continued to think along those lines.

Later, while brushing my hair, I saw Karan waking up behind me in the mirror. He looked around, and saw me standing in front of the mirror. He looked at me with tender eyes and walked towards me. He held me from behind and kissed my hair and whispered 'good morning'. His eyes revealed the same passion he had shown at night. Maybe that was love. I could not tell.

He picked his bag and left the apartment. Before he left, he saw the bite marks he had on his neck and smirked. It felt like a smirk of victory.

Not wanting much time to think, I dressed.

When I stepped out of the bathroom, I peeked to look for him but he had left. That day I didn't go to work, pondering on my decision. It had been seven hours since he left, I was sitting alone in the balcony. I had declared to myself with a tone of finality that this was my decision. I kept walking back and forth in the room from the balcony, repeating the same line to myself with finality and certainty.

Next few weeks went just like that—violent sex and early morning runs. I had toned my body quite well with the arduous schedule I was putting it through.

The new office turned out to be lucky for me. I was promoted and finally, I was a manager. However, this was clearly just a designation change and it made no major change to my job profile. With my raise, I decided to start investing. I was always a prudent investor but now I could become courageous too.

I was breezing through life like an eagle breezing through its territory. Life was good.

Suddenly, something happened…

While enjoying our evening espresso and casually chatting with Karan, I faced a roadblock. A roadblock worth a mention.

'So what do you do with your extra salary?' It was a spur of the moment question asked by Karan. It was out of his character, because he didn't discuss finances. It had never come up in a conversation before. This was out of the ordinary. I disliked discussing my financial matters openly. It was personal and I liked it to remain personal.

Naturally my face bore the impressions of distaste at his query, but I said, 'Nothing much.' There it was, a curt reply to a raucous question. I have been managing my finances since I was 16. All these years and no one had ever asked me what I did with my money. Calming my nerves, I wondered why he had asked. I contemplated asking him the same and it now seemed reasonable to ask him.

'What do you do?' I felt confident enough to ask something so personal after he had asked me so casually, like he was ordering a coffee.

He shrugged and replied, 'Well, I don't do much. Actually, I don't feel very comfortable discussing my personal finances.'

There was a sharp silence in the room when he spoke.

I was fuming but my face showed no creases, no reactions. My face was like that of an angel, but inside I was quashing my feelings. There wasn't any explanation of why I didn't react, but I didn't. At that instant, I realized that I feared his wrath. Now I knew two experiences of love—one being love itself and the other was fear.

'Am I supposed to be scared of my partner? Love does come with the fear of losing the other person.' But I couldn't differentiate whether I was afraid of losing him or of his anger. I had seen his anger before and even though I had placed it in a small corner of my memory, it existed. I chained that memory inside so it wouldn't rear its ugly head. But it's there. It was very prominent and loud. I dared not wake it up because I felt threatened. I'm unable to let go of him, so I'd rather let go of that memory.

But the mind plays games; it will vehemently remind you of the things you want to forget.

He was still talking and this time it was closer to the point. 'I was wondering if we should have a joint account.'

I had a blank face, not being able to comprehend his question. I replayed the question in my head again and then again. But the outcome was still blank.

'Oh!' I said.

After reading my lack of a response, he continued, 'Maybe we should put aside some amount every month for our future. I can put in double the amount of what you deposit.'

I was flattered, but the idea of a joint account was intimidating. His way of proposing was unique. Instead of the cliches—'I love you', 'Will you marry me?'—he had asked for a joint bank account. I couldn't crush his dreams by saying that I was unsure about the future of our relationship when he was building a house with me in his head. I couldn't tell him that I thought he was a psychopath, when clearly, on numerous occasions, I had violent sex with him. I couldn't tell him I didn't believe him enough to spend my hard-earned money on him, so I found the best solution. A lie.

'I don't save enough. My expenses cover my salary. I live by the day.'

That was it. Now my relationship with him had turned into a Karan-pleasing game. I stopped saying the truth and found relief in pleasing him even if I had to lie.

I tried to avoid talking about finance with Karan. Later, I sat alone in the dark, too fatigued to get up to switch on the lights. I remembered another dark night. There was a massive power cut swathing the entire city with a thick blanket of unsettling darkness.

I thought of doing something different from what I always did. It was a storm-swept, rain-drenched evening. The storm and the rain had claimed a lot of shanties and awnings...

I decided to meet Deva for coffee.

I sat at the same table where we used to while planning the new office opening. He ordered his usual, and I ordered double espresso shots. I needed the extra kick after that gruelling conversation with my boyfriend. As usual, with Deva it was effortless. He was my much-needed coffee. I wondered if I'd stopped spending as much time with him after our project. We laughed, spoke about life, and discussed random theories.

The storms brimmed over our cups as we braved the torrential rain. Later we swore at our bosses and dished out advice to each other on diplomatic handling of office politics...

A slippery road, a stalled windscreen wiper and torrents of rain. The winds howled on our faces. The sky wept with us. Yet I could not help but notice how beautifully ordinary Deva was. I was the one who ignored him.

I realized we both needed each other. Then Deva spoke. 'When I'm with you, I don't feel the pressure of being judged. I don't have to prove myself to you. It doesn't feel naked around you. Everywhere else, people look at me with ugly or pitiful eyes. You see worth in me, and I feel worthy when I'm around you.'

He paused for some time and then continued, 'Don't get me wrong, as much as I like you, I know I can't have you. And I also know you are in love with Karan. All I want is to be your friend. I see the sparkle in your eyes when you are with me, and I feel the same light with you. It's rare and rather lucky to find this kind of union.'

He took another deep breath and spoke again, 'I know all this is very hard to process and maybe you must wonder what a nut I am but I rarely speak my heart like this. I am saying all this because I don't want to lose you. You, again, must think I am crazy. But you are the first person in my life who has accepted me effortlessly. And I want to hand myself over to you.'

He looked up, as though thinking, and said, 'This is the first time I've asked someone for something.' He was lost in thought again. He looked like a kid trying to remember something. He kept looking up and squeezing his eyes shut.

'Yes, the first time. First time!'

And the tension in the air vanished; he had a glow on his face, like he'd accomplished a big deal. He must have rehearsed this a million times before telling me. And now his face looked relieved but apprehensive of what I thought.

I smiled, then laughed, and then finally spoke, 'Deva, all these things are not to be said, but felt. This was the case for me too. You have been my rock and my friend. Your unconditional support has been a huge pillar of strength. You are the reason I think that if everyone in the world abandons me, I know I can turn to you anytime. Thank you so much for being there for me without asking for anything in return. You have given me much more than what I have or can give you. So, I am very grateful to you for being you!

'Please don't change. Stay the wonderful person you are. Don't let others crush you and your charm. You are better than most out there. Show your real self to others and everyone will be in love with you, just like I am.

'And now coming to the point…I think we should get you a girlfriend.'

My eyes were twinkling. And I had a perfect plan.

Deva smirked back but his embarrassment couldn't be hidden. I knew his first choice would be me, but I was taken for now. I wished I had known him before and our future could be different.

But now I had a mission. It excited me to be useful, my latent need to please someone kicked in again. Then I named many people from the office, some I struck off, and some he. We were enjoying this new hunt we were on. We struck off names in each department, and then suddenly, I had the best idea of the year, or maybe the decade.

My pitch was higher than anyone else in the cafe.

'Saira' I said and my eyes glowed. He looked at me. He was taken aback. It was a radical idea—no one dared look at Saira. She was always grumpy and quiet, some thought she was depressed. But Saira was the best person in the office. She was kind and very helpful. However, her demeanour wasn't desirable and she snapped whenever she encountered stupidity, so people mostly stayed away.

Deva was thinking. 'Why would she want to be with me?' he paused for some time, as if calculating. 'No. I think this idea of finding a girlfriend isn't working. I'm happy being single at 35. I have had only one relationship, five years back. I don't think I can get back into that self-incriminating hellhole.'

He was going back on his word! But I was not going to give up. 'Why? Saira is an amazing person. She is educated and professionally settled. She does not seek boyfriends everywhere she goes. She is level-headed. She's got a brain. I don't understand.' I looked at him, puzzled.

We sipped our coffee and stared at the cars passing by. We saw schoolkids walking with bags on their back and water bottles on their shoulders, jumping and carefree. We saw a newly-wed couple sharing a chuski and talking to each other. We saw college kids smoking. The shops across the road cried for repair, which seemed impossible though, considering the broken tiles and eroded iron frames. The road in the front was dotted with numerous potholes that had become small pools where frogs had settled, croaking happily during the rains. Buses, long and swanky and bright red, went past us, creating a brief storm near the shops and sent odd bits of paper, dried shrivelled leaves, plastic bags and clouds of dirt flying, blinding the few pairs of eyes that were present there at those decrepit shops. Only two buses halted at this bus stop all days a week, and they went in opposite directions. One in the morning and the other late in the afternoon.

I wondered why sales here were low despite passengers getting off at this point. I started the calculations. The place was visited by rushing, dragging feet of the young and old, showered by bits of paper and plastic packets, to be preserved for the express storms to carry away routinely. The only beauty about the place was the flowering gulmohar tree and the greyish-blue soft lines of hillocks far away in the skyline. The man who begged at the bend of the road was the only permanent aspect of this station. Then there was this other man who gazed at the faraway hills and did odd jobs for the shop owners. And when he was tired, he lay down under the voluminous gulmohar tree, collecting and smelling the flowers that occasionally dropped on the ground. He managed to eat meals using the paltry sum of money the shop owners gave him.

I was shaken from my brooding when Deva said, 'What do you see there? You are an intense person.'

I looked at him and we burst out laughing.

'I'm scared of her,' he said. He had a twinkle in his eyes when he said that. He was embarrassed and blushing. I had my answer. Now I had a new job: to get the two best people I know together. I was already scheming

Deva seemed reluctant. In his place, I would too. Saira was a terror to everyone, whether she knew them or not. There was something about her that evoked fear. She came across as a loner, but that was the prime reason we had become friends—we were both loners. And if I could change, she surely could too. I wanted her to feel the happiness I felt with Karan. She might have reservations after what had happened to me, but life is all about taking and giving things a second chance.

Deva, almost imagining himself with Saira, nervously said, 'Maybe we should find someone else?' His face was red with awkwardness. Knowing how close I was to Saira, he must have marshalled real courage.

As I could hear his heartbeat—it was louder than the honks of the cars outside—I decided to give him time to process this new development. It was a beautiful evening so we walked to the beach and sat down to listen to the sound of the waves. The beach was crowded with a large group of older men conducting their laughing club.

'I wonder how someone can laugh on demand?' he said, making a sweeping inquiry.

'I can,' I said, fixing my gaze at the horizon, answering as if I was talking to the wind. 'I like the innocence of the act. I like the aura it creates. They aren't just helping themselves, they are also helping others around them. It immediately puts you in a good mood. Look around, that kid who was crying has stopped crying now.'

'He stopped crying because he was scared of their loud laughter.'

We looked at each other and burst out laughing again. It was a funny sight and very inspiring at the same time.

We sat there for a while longer, letting the breeze touch our face. The wind threw droplets of ocean water carrying the scent of the universe on our face like some mist. It was lovely.

Deva got chatty with some kids and was racing with them on the sand. Of course, he lost miserably but the sparkle in his eyes was childlike and his smile was timeless.

He came back gasping for breath. 'How old are you again?' I asked and we were once again in splits. I hadn't laughed so much in a long time. It felt good to feel good.

Then, he walked me home. We stopped at every chaat hawker on the way, eating and chatting away and enjoying each other's company.

I stayed awake that night, mesmerised. The night had curled into itself, like whirls of black smoke emanating from the chimneys of a factory. Its darkness took on different shapes and forms and spread widely in all directions. I came out to the balcony and looked up.

The sky had disappeared. All that lay before me, above and around me was a thick sheet of darkness. It wrapped me within itself. I saw some bats gyrating above, their seemingly limbless torsos moving as they flapped their joined wings. The night danced along with the bats in a perfect synchronized choreography. And just then, beams of white joined them. I saw a lonely figure silhouetted against the darkness of the night on my neighbour's balcony.

11

My mind raced to find ways to get Deva and Saira together. It wasn't a difficult job. They were both connected to each other through me and now Deva was on board at least. Saira wasn't likely to be wooed by gifts and gestures. She was different and all she cared about was stability and respect. She was not for the weak-hearted. She loved hard and also hated hard. She was a beautiful person inside out. But all the ways to her heart were closed. She hated the idea of me dating someone, and for her, it would be a sin to see someone. She had lost a lot in love and she didn't have the courage to lose more. Her experiences in love with her family and a lover were harsh, so she devoted her love to herself. But Deva would be perfect for her.

I would have liked it to happen organically, but that seemed like a wild fantasy. So, I pulled my socks up.

While I had been plotting for some time in my head, I noticed that Deva had put his best shirt on for the day and it made me nervous. I hoped I would do justice by him. I put my best foot forward for the sake of Deva's new pink shirt.

It had amused me when he wore it on the day the new office had opened and it amused me today. No, not because it was pink, but because he had no colour coordination. He paired that baby pink shirt with dark blue pants and a brown belt. Luckily, his shoes were brown and it was a saving grace. But if you want to know what not to wear, all one had to do was to look at Deva. He was a walking guide. Saira would have to be the one to break it to him about his dressing sense. She could take him shopping.

And there it was! My first idea to get them together. As much as Saira hated shopping, Deva had no clue about it whatsoever. This could be a good way to start.

During our afternoon coffee break on the terrace, Saira and I were just looking at the sun about to set when Deva walked in. I had planned for their paths to intersect, but Saira didn't need to know. It was our secret.

With the rays of the setting sun falling on Deva, his colour combination didn't look all that bad. He smiled at us and then looked down. There was something about his demeanour that made me realize how insecure he was about himself. His self-doubts were evident. He didn't have anyone to tell him how good he was. He needed someone like Saira and she needed someone like him.

'What are your plans for the weekend, Saira?' As casually as I could, I posed the question.

She raised her eyebrow, wondering why I asked. But she let it fly. After I had got back together with Karan, she had been aloof with me. I might be imagining it, but there wasn't much I could do about it. I was in love with Karan, or so I believed. Deva was nervous around Saira. He even used to call her 'Hitler' before he got to know her. It was justified for him to be petrified.

I asked again as no one seemed to reply.

'This Sunday, let's go around town. Shopping?' I heard myself talking about shopping and almost laughed. Saira was likely to notice that something was fishy. But because of my questionable behaviour lately, she took this with a pinch of salt.

'Let's all meet on Sunday. 11.00 a.m. at Colaba, Cafe Mondegar.' And to make it amply clear, I added, 'Why don't you get your car, Deva? So we can go where we want to after shopping.'

Saira immediately looked up. She gave me an elusive look to ask why he had been invited, but I ignored. I quickly threw my cup in the trash and walked away. I didn't want to encourage any questions. I had a smirk on my face while walking down to my desk. This first win felt good.

On Sunday, Deva and Saira showed up right on time outside Cafe Mondegar and waited for me.

I had a different plan. I had already decided that I would not show up. And I did just that!

At 11.20 a.m., the first message came like clockwork.

'Where the hell are you?' Saira's impatience was oozing out of the phone.

But I decided to give it some more time. I was busy polishing off books from my bookshelf. I had planned a relaxing day with my books at home. Unless Saira was very upset, I wouldn't join them. The vibe of her message was as expected, so I put my feet up and waited for my phone to ring.

Then, exactly in ten minutes, my phone rang again. Deva was smart enough to understand my plan ahead and he was surprisingly cool.

I picked the phone after four rings, and used my urgent voice. Then, I said, 'Hello, I'm soooooo sorry.' I wasn't impressed by my own acting skills. I could do better. So I added some spice to it and said, 'I hurt my leg soooooo badly.'

Saira fell quiet. There was an eerie silence. For a second, I was forced to think that I should go and salvage Deva from her wrath, but I had already lied. And if I gave in, she'd be smart enough to understand my ulterior motive. I stood my ground and waited patiently to hear her voice.

'Does that mean you aren't coming?' she said. A matter of fact question posed by this practical friend of mine. If I said 'yes' she would go back home, spoiling my plan. I played my cards.

'Maybe you can start shopping, and I'll try to ice this.'

Momentarily, I was certain she would refuse, but surprisingly, she replied. 'Sure, call us. We will be waiting at Cafe Mondegar, since shopping was only on your agenda,' she said blatantly. It made me consider whether she had already sensed a whiff of my plan. I said a small prayer for Deva, and went back to my books.

My phone beeped and I was sure it was Saira but the voice on the other side was Karan. He said, 'I miss you. I know that you told me you wanted a quiet weekend. But I was wondering if I could come by and make no noise but just be there with you?'

This was probably one of the most romantic things

someone had ever said to me. I blushed like a teenager. I felt butterflies in my stomach. He had spoken so softly, probably while lying down in his bed. I could barely think straight with Karan beseeching me.

∞

At the cafe, Saira and Deva ordered a coffee and sat there wondering what they could do next. Deva understood that this was the plan to begin with, so he played along. He was very interesting and had a lot of fun facts to share with her. He was always ready to chat when it was one-on-one. He didn't take much time before pulling Saira into the conversation. Coffee turned into breakfast and then into lunch. This was an unexpected but a welcome twist.

They sat there and finally Saira said, 'This b**** Meera is not going to come now. She has one hurt leg today, tomorrow she will have two.'

Deva meekly smiled, while being terrified within.

They spent another three hours there together. Finally, I sent a message to her phone. 'I'm sorry. The swelling hasn't subsided. I'd rather rest. Love you.' This was the first time I had told Saira that I love her. She was the first one I felt like saying it to. She and I had a special connection. I hadn't felt it before with anyone else and I wanted to treasure it like it was my goldmine.

Saira wasn't happy with today's events, but she realized that Deva wasn't that bad either. In fact, she was happy to be with Deva.

Minutes turned into hours, discussing their lives. Saira

had always been a loner and making friends wasn't in her nature. However, deep inside, she was happy to spend time with a new friend.

At the end of the day, she called me and said that she missed me. But she also thanked me for helping her find a friend in Deva. She cursed me for not showing up. Then she showered random praises on Deva. After I hung up, I realized that I had found the best friend I had been searching for since childhood. It's better late than never. There is always a first time for everything. And this was mine.

After unwinding with a glass of wine and salad with Karan, I got a message from Deva and my heart melted. 'You have no idea what you have done for me today. No one has been as kind as you. In fact, no one noticed me before you. At some point, I stopped noticing myself. But you have been my guiding angel from the time I knew you. May god bless you for your goodness that you spread and you surely have a heart of gold. You are the friend I never dreamed I could have. Good night.'

That night, past midnight—that's what I thought the time was—I had a dream. A vivid dream, almost real. I felt every emotion in the dream. I could feel my heart sink.

I saw my mom in the dream. I had never seen my mom as she had died when I was born. This always saddened me. In my dream, I didn't see her face. But something in the dream told me that this was my mother.

We lived in medieval times in clay huts. Or maybe, we were just very poor. Hungry and thirsty, three little bodies, including my own, sat shrunk and huddled. We whimpered on the narrow strip of land where a woman was cooking something on the fire. The shanty was by a filthy, stinking canal. A male lay inside on a thin tattered mattress they called their bed. I looked on helplessly but the woman had no face. It was cold so I kept trying to get closer to the fire, to get some warmth. She was wearing an orange sari and the end was wrapped around her head. I was wearing a frock and my legs were bare. I kept trying to get closer to her or to the fire and she kept pushing me away with her elbow. I could see other kids around the fire, probably siblings. Their sunken deep eyes were lined with dark circles so black that they looked like stale smudged kohl. I could make out that we were extremely poor. She spoke to her children with her eyes, without uttering a word. The eldest understood, and pacified the younger ones, including me.

Finally, I moved with a jump, ignoring my mother's nudges and I saw myself in the pot. She was cooking my face in the earth oven. I was aghast and horror-struck. I couldn't believe my eyes. My face on the stove scared me stiff. I did not move.

I tried touching my face and couldn't feel it. I wondered how anything like this was possible. I tried to call out to my mother but she didn't hear me, instead she kept on telling me, 'Meera, move away from the stove. You will get burnt.'

I tried telling her I was being burnt, but I didn't feel a thing and nor did my voice come out. I was completely choked.

I was crying but no tears came out. I pulled at my mother to look at me and see my face but she stood like a stone, motionless. She constantly looked at the stove and didn't turn back even once. Then I heard it—a loud scream. And I opened my eyes, gasping for breath. I was sweating.

Karan had woken up in the middle of the night. The windows were open and there was enough light coming in from the street below. He watched me in shocked silence, frozen and agape with confusion. I was too scared to move. I was trembling all over. I turned on the other side and hugged my pillow tight and wept silently.

Karan held me tight as he saw me shaking with fear and disbelief. He simply stroked my hair and I buried my face into his chest. And he heard me repeating, 'It was a bad dream, a very bad dream'.

That night, he slept holding me tight, keeping me guarded.

After that nightmarish dream, I was composed and in control of my worlds but I was baffled, confused and tormented from within. There were gaps now, hidden but revealing at the same time. I looked for myself in the gaps. I saw a faceless figure in the mirror, a dislocated childhood striving to adapt reflected there. A loner, a misfit in the measured system called a harmonious life, who has never had a world to call her own. Belonging to two worlds, one for the people to see and another hidden, dark with a past. I burnt alone, like the flame of a flickering lamp.

The next few days were a blur. Deva and Saira had hit it off and I started getting fewer messages from Deva, although he still kept close contact with me, like always. I did not know that Saira and Deva lived in adjacent blocks in the same locality and met every day. They were closer than friends already, maybe already lovers. They visited art galleries, attended musical soirees and went to movies together. Deva and Saira travelled, dreamed and breathed together. They complemented each other, binding and releasing, sailing together.

I focused on mending my relationship with Karan by putting the negative thoughts about him aside. I wanted a clean slate. I wanted to forget all his narcissistic behaviour and give him another chance.

Deva and Saira were at our usual spot, drinking coffee, when Karan and I walked in. One thing led to another and all of us were planning our weekend

'How about we celebrate Karan's birthday?' Deva said. It was surprising that he knew about Karan's birthday.

That threw a curve ball at me, but I let it slide. I was being overly sensitive. Karan gave me a look to ask if I was okay. Of course, I was okay. He didn't know I was on a mission to make sure Saira and Deva get together. And this was a chance to get them closer. I never knew I would have to play the role of a matchmaker. Momentarily, I wondered how my life had changed after Karan, how I had become much more tolerant and less expecting. He was moulding me, but my core still remained untouched. On the other hand, I was making him more resilient too. Never in his wildest dreams had he imagined inviting Deva and Saira for his birthday. For that matter, never did I imagine he would be open about us in front of our colleagues. But I accepted it. Growing in a relationship is key to its longevity.

That night Saira decided to come and stay for the weekend. She was in high spirits. I could see her dreamy eyes fluttering. She was like a butterfly. She was in love, whether she accepted it or not. She was happy and smiled more. We opened a bottle of wine and sat on the balcony and contemplated how life had changed for us.

'Can I ask you something?' Saira said. Her eyes were dreamy from the wine and love. 'How could you go back to Karan after what he did to you? I mean how could you forgive him?'

I smiled and said, 'I never forgave him, I only accepted him with his faults. Of course, I want to believe it was a one-time occurrence. A strange instance of violence. I have convinced myself about it. And I will give life a chance, I will give love one more chance. It's a gamble I'm willing to take.'

Saira took a deep breath and looked at the sky.

She said, 'I never knew I would say this, but I think I understand what you say. Once you are fond of someone, you want to accept his or her limitations too.'

A voice from above us spoke. 'That blind faith and bullshit!'

I looked up and saw Abhi. I smiled at him.

12

On the day of Karan's birthday, sipping on my favourite drink, I sat in the corner of the room. Music was blasting out of the house. It was too loud, and dare I say deafening! I was sitting and wondering if it would be okay to mute it for some time. After dancing for a long time, Karan was sloshed. Everyone was tanked up. He kept doing the same step, again and again. It was a sight for sore eyes. Very rarely do you see people in their element, throwing their hair in the air, not being judged. Karan's college buddies were there too. I found them interesting.

As planned, Deva was dancing with Saira and she wasn't complaining. In fact, she was in a different world. For once, she didn't want to tell me why I shouldn't be with Karan. She had given up. She was so transfixed by Deva that she couldn't see anything further. From the time she had entered, her eyes hadn't left him. He too was glued to her without touching her. She was also hammered, and seeing Saira like that made me drink less. I wanted someone to be in control, in case anything happened. Too many drunk people in the same house would spell danger. The bungalow had been rented by Karan and it wasn't in a secluded area. The closest bus stop was a twenty-minute walk from the premises and it was impossible to find a cab.

There was a counter for food and drinks but no one seemed to be eating. Everyone flooded the drinks table. It was self-service, so the drunks spilled more than they poured. There was one guy who remained suspiciously sane. Karan's school friend, Aakash. Karan introduced him briefly to me, just for the sake of it. I didn't put much thought to it either, but Aakash kept looking at me. He sent some signals to me indicating that he wanted to talk, but he seemed aloof, like he couldn't make up his mind.

He came around when Karan went to the restroom. He quickly came by and said something. It rang in my ears.

'Does he take care of you?' he asked.

I wasn't able to process the question fast enough, and I didn't think anyone would even ask me such a question. I was perplexed and did not know if he was even talking to me. Then I gathered that he must be drunk, but I had been watching him. I had noted that he didn't drink much. He just toyed with a glass in his hand and that was all.

So, I looked up with a confused expression. I wondered whether he would realize that he was talking to the wrong person, but he was persistent.

'Do you know him well?'

Another question, equally hard to interpret. Then Karan came out of the restroom and Aakash fled. I didn't see him again throughout the night. He disappeared into thin air, but he left a lump in my throat. He said a lot without saying much. I tried to decipher his words from every possible angle, and every angle seemed to carry bad news. I tried to recall how Karan had introduced us. It was fluid and short. 'One of my close childhood friends,' he said. They were different. Karan was breezy but Aakash seemed bitter.

But I was thinking too much.

I wanted to enjoy the party and keep a level head. I lurched over to Deva. He was the only good dancer on the dance floor. He had taken over the stage with his Punjabi steps. Looking at him, one could say that it's not in the detail, but happiness is found in chaos. When there isn't no order, there is creativity. And he had no order to his dance moves. His dance moves were random, like him. Saira was swaying with him like they were lovers in Bollywood, dancing around trees. They were adorable, if not lovable. Seeing Saira like this made my heart skip. I had missed this part with Karan and there it was. I was comparing.

'But there is nothing wrong with comparing,' I told myself.

Everyone in the room saw Deva's vibe and Saira's jive. They were the stars of the evening. They swayed to the Bollywood numbers and rocked on Ariana Grande. There wasn't a single song they weren't excited about. They whooped at every dance number. I saw Deva slipping his hand around Saira's waist. I'm sure if he were sober, he wouldn't dare make the moves he was making now. And I was sure that Saira wouldn't loosen up as much if she weren't sloshed. Then again, they weren't so sloshed as to not understand what was happening.

The booze only helped them loosen up and take a few bold steps, which otherwise wouldn't have happened.

'Are you enjoying yourself?' Karan asked, smiling and slurping a drink.

I gave him a kind smile, not wanting to reveal all the things I was thinking. It made me think about how much an average person can hide during a conversation with another. More is hidden than said—perhaps a 30:70 ratio. It's well around the normal range. If someone actually spoke their mind, they would be in danger of being considered a lunatic. Thoughts are best kept in the mind. I had learned this early in my life and through difficultly. Now I believed in the idiom: 'Thou shalt keep thy thoughts to thyself.'

'Loving it! But it's your birthday, so you should be the one enjoying yourself more.' I gave him a quick response and was impressed by my communication skills.

He slurped some more and came closer to kiss me. Believe it or not, it felt unappealing. He was sweaty and looked like a Bollywood villain about to pounce on me without my consent. I pulled my lips out as a pout and kissed his lips with a bare minimum touch.

I learned a trick, I felt. And I intend to use it in the future.

I hated public displays of affection. I had enjoyed his attention the other night at the office opening as he was declaring our relationship, and it had felt special. But otherwise, affection is private, not public.

I saw that Saira was now dancing in Deva's arms. My job was done. The wonders of good music and alcohol, I thought. It could do miracles one might never imagine even though, sometimes, it could also be a cause of unhappiness.

I was getting cozy, leaning into the mood of the party. I walked out for a stroll around the house. The cool breeze brushed past my face. The sky was full of stars; it was a clear night with the moon at its best. It was imperfectly circular, bright yellow in colour, woken from its beauty sleep. It looked like a young bride, shy behind the clouds, peeking through to look for the lover. The stars were twinkling for her to be able to see her lover.

There were rows of houses in front of me. I saw elongated shadows of objects swimming in dim light from every house. Through open windows, slammed doors and solid walls, life danced in liquid movements. The shadows circled the night and swayed along to the music that played in my head. I yearned to join them.

I was there, in the centre, one with the night. I was dancing. I was looking, at my city and the entire sleeping planet. I saw myself too—a teensy-weensy black dot, no bigger than an ant. I felt the vastness of the universe.

I sat on the side of the house. There was a stone bench with something engraved on it and many things scribbled on it. The scribbles were more visible than the engravings.

That's when I heard someone walk out with hurried steps. It was one of the girls rushing to the bathroom. She looked sloshed (like most of them) and one man followed right behind her. Probably to help! But something felt off about the whole scene. I felt a bit responsible. I had to help her. I was mindful of the fact that the man may take this as an opportunity in the dark.

I tiptoed on my heels, cautiously, not wanting to alert anyone. I wondered whether she needed someone other than the man to help. I heard something rustling and I went further. I saw them both and realized what had made me feel so strange earlier. The man was holding her by her waist while she was trying to puke. She was resisting him. Looking closely, he was fondling her. And she wasn't in her senses.

I was fuming with anger, but I looked closely. I hoped I had been imagining it. But again, I could see that he was touching her all over while saying that everything would be alright. His words were kind, but his hands moved like that of a devil.

She didn't understand, she was too drunk to understand.

'What the hell are you doing?' I screamed loudly.

He was alerted and immediately moved his hands away from her body. She was hunched trying to vomit.

'Nothing!' As a reflex, he screamed louder than me.

'I know what you were doing!' I screamed back.

Karan and some other friends came out running on hearing the commotion.

'What happened, Meera?' He spoke to me rudely. 'What is this drama about?' he asked. I could hear his anger.

I narrowed my eyes, not wanting to throw a fit of rage. I ignored his rudeness. I went into a defensive mode and started explaining what had happened. Karan was sloshed and drunk, and he gave me a cold look. Then he looked away. He wanted me to shut up. He refused to listen. He kept wondering why I was screaming and spoiling his party. He held my hand harder than I liked and it was hurting me.

I wanted to tell him that. I wanted to yell at him for his behaviour. I didn't like the way his nails were piercing into my skin. But my attention was on the girl standing there, still holding her stomach and that man still standing right next to her.

He saw Karan's reaction and smirked. It was his victory. It felt as if he saw through Karan and my relationship. I felt naked all of a sudden. I remembered that night when Karan had attacked me. He was drunk that night too. But there was no legitimate explanation for his behaviour. 'Will he react in the same way now that he is drunk again?'

I pushed his hand away gently, and without drama, stomped off. I safely put my hand over the girl's shoulder and took her inside the noisy living room. I took her upstairs to a bedroom. Karan had claimed it for our after-party. I gave her a bottle of water and made her sit down.

'Are you feeling better?' I put my hand on her hair and stroked it.

She looked at me and started crying. She was a young girl. She had come to have fun. It had probably turned into the worst night of her life.

She cried some more and said, 'I'm fine now. Please go to the party. I don't want to spoil your evening.'

I gave her a faint smile and continued stroking her hair. I got some food for her to eat, some naan to soak up the alcohol.

'Can I ask you something?' I said. I didn't want to live in self-doubt so I asked. 'Was he trying to take advantage of you?'

Her eyes narrowed and I saw tears rolling down her eyes.

She answered in the affirmative. Karan's behaviour had made me wonder whether I was imagining things. I had to make sure of my sanity.

'I kept telling him to move away but he was following me the whole night. Trying to dance close to me. I kept telling him to stay away. But he found me at my most vulnerable.' She paused. 'Then I felt his hand creeping on my waist but I didn't move it. I didn't react to my brain telling me to stop him. I froze.'

I looked at her and stroked her hair again.

She rushed to the toilet, and kept going back and forth to vomit and rest. She seemed better after every visit to the toilet. She sat down and sobbed a lot. But the damage was done. This nightmare would haunt her forever.

All I could do was say, 'It will be okay!' even though I wasn't sure where this would take her. I blamed her too for being reckless, but the onus was on the man who was in his senses and had taken advantage of her inebriation.

There was a knock on the door.

It was Karan!

I sat there. I watched him come close, not knowing what to expect from him. I continued to gaze at the crying woman. She looked at me, knowing Karan was here to talk to me. She rose to her feet and excused herself, but I held her hand and signalled for her to stay. She seemed uncomfortable with Karan in the room, and had probably sensed his mood. But she stayed where I told her to and didn't move.

'Can I talk to you, Meera?' Karan said in an authoritative tone.

I looked up. If only my look could kill him. He stood next to me and continued. 'What was that downstairs?' he asked.

I calmly said, 'What did it look like to you?'

This exchange was making the woman uncomfortable, I could sense it.

'Why were you screaming?' he asked, now raging.

'Why are you asking me again? You have asked me when it happened. But instead of finding out the truth you threw a fit. Insulted me in front of all your guests. And without knowing what happened.' I paused. 'You simply assumed I was in the wrong and you didn't even ask me?'

I was hurt and it was evident in my tone. I had forgiven him many times, and he kept repeating his mistakes.

'He tried to touch me inappropriately. If it wasn't for Meera, he would have molested me in my drunken state.' The girl spoke up for me.

I looked at him with anger and rage. I would never forgive him, I told myself.

Listening to all this commotion, Saira and Deva came upstairs looking for us.

Karan was screaming on the top of his voice. 'You don't understand, you always think I'm the bad guy. Just because I allow you to do what you want—'

I raised my hand asking him to stop with fire in my eyes.

'Did you say you "allow" me?' I repeated. 'Did you just say you "allow" me?'

I stormed out of the room and walked into the night. Saira and Deva were beside me.

Typhoons aren't always sudden. One can forecast and foresee them. The lovers beside me were caught in one and met it with undeniable surprise. Some storms are sudden. They emerge from the blue sky and one can be caught unawares. The window shutters slam and doors bang at the assault of a ravaging blast. A problem enters our life like a tiny piece of dust in the eye.

Such was this episode in my life.

No, the incident wasn't sudden. I had forgiven Karan too easily earlier and probably I would forgive him again. I had lost my path, I was blind and greedy for affection. I feared being lonely again.

Now I had lost my self-respect.

As expected, he pleaded and I forgave him, again, branding this incident as well as a one-off thing. And I knew why I kept doing this, over and over. It was because I had accepted him as he was.

I was weak around him.

13

The banquet hall was well lit. Marigold veils were flowing in the air, dancing in unison with the mood. The kids with their colourful kurtis were running and playing around gleefully. The classical music blaring from the huge sound boxes was loud enough, and the repartee moved up through the hall. The stages were intricately designed in the middle of the palatial garden. The rituals were to be held by the breezy seashore. Shehnai music flooded the place and all the trees donned fairy lights. The entire area was bright. Even to me, the bustle of people conveyed that a night of grand celebration was underway. Women in colourful saris and lehengas were adjusting their hair with their henna-clad hands. With a jiggle of their bangles they kept smiling at one another.

At the door of the banquet hall, it read: Karan weds Meera.
And below that it read: Deva weds Saira.

Yes, Saira was hitched to Deva. It had been a pleasure to get them together and now, finally, I would see them bound by wedding vows. And Karan and me, maybe we were meant to be together. His idiosyncrasies and mine matched.

I paused and sighed. I again looked at the boards. I was getting married today.

As I entered the wedding hall, my vision was blurry. It was not because of tears but I struggled under the weight of the heavy makeup. My head felt heavy because of the large amount of hair spray on my hair. I tried to carry the weight of my gaudy embroidered ghagra (gifted by my in-laws), and balanced myself on my pencil heels.

I took a full five minutes to step out of the car. It was not because I was heavy, but because of the heavy outfit. It was made to 'fit the occasion', according to Karan's mother. Sure, it fitted the occasion. The amount of cloth and gaudy golden embroidery on it, if converted into gold, would be enough to feed a generation. As I walked out of the car, my ghagra dragged and swept the place.

God bless Karan's cousin, who quickly came to my rescue and helped me pull it up. Except she pulled it way too high.

She looked at me in horror, thinking that I would thrash her, but I simply giggled. I was in no mood to thrash anyone. At this moment, the one who was being thrashed was me!

I wore a line of coloured bindis on my forehead; it looked lovely on the foreheads of Bollywood heroines, but on my tiny forehead and dark skin, it looked like I had been struck by lightning. I dared not look at the mirror because if I did, it would break. I didn't recognize myself when I glanced over the car to see my reflection.

The place looked splendid and I looked kitschy in comparison. Of course, it was because I had selected the decor and Karan's mother had selected every piece of my clothing, ornaments and makeup. I only adored the henna on my hand. The artist was talented, and she did intricate work on my palms. This was the first time I had put henna on my hand and it was special.

I lived up to the role of a traditional Indian bride. I was not supposed to do anything but obey what the mother-in-law asked me to do.

The only good thing I wore was the ring that Karan had given me when he had proposed. He had good taste, but his mother would make me wear fake stones if it would make her family look rich. I felt the first instance of dismay when I went shopping with her for my ghagra. She did not bother to ask about my choice and taste. I wondered whether I was there only for my measurements. She didn't ask me what colour or what style I wanted. Once, meekly, I tried to point at a baby pink and lightly embroidered dupatta. She looked at me like I had abused her. Scared that I had enraged her, I refrained from talking. I was made to try on the most outrageous salwar kameez and ghagra at the stores we visited. She spent a lot of money, but it made me look horrendous. Their purchases were clearly a show of wealth. They were lacking in taste.

The nightmares had continued when I went with Karan's mother to a relative's house. She told me to put the dupatta over my head. I was appalled but amused by her stupidity. I knew this act had to be put on while she was around, and then I could live my life my way. I reckoned that it was important to make adjustments, and hence I let it slide.

'But should I have let it slide?'

As I entered, a bunch of Karan's relatives rushed towards me, like I was on fire. But they were simply excited. Sometimes it's hard to decipher whether Punjabis are excited or scared. They can have the same set of facial expressions in both the circumstances. An instant giggle escaped me. They wondered about it, but didn't put too much thought to it. Their excitement for someone else's wedding was beyond my understanding, but I played along and I played well. I felt happy as I looked at their happy faces.

After being transported to another room, I quickly messaged Saira. Then I struggled to put my dupatta over the other dupatta over the shawl-like dupatta over the dupatta that went over my head. It felt like a mountaineering excursion. But I made it. Finally, appreciating my henna once again, I sent her a quick message.

'Where the hell are you?'

And the reply came back quicker than the speed of light.

'Right next door. Come to the balcony,' she replied.

I ran towards the balcony, pulling my ghagra up, a little higher than my knee. It felt like heavy-weight lifting. But I would do anything to steal a glance of my best friend on her wedding day, the same day as mine. That had been my only condition when Karan had proposed to me: we get married in the same place and on the same day as Deva and Saira. If I was to jump, I'd rather jump in company.

Saira was furious at me for this. Deva had to propose to her right after as well, not that he minded. They were in a good place. Though they were more in love than us, they needed the extra nudge.

I wonder why I had said 'yes' to Karan, and even today, I couldn't find a concrete answer. Maybe, at the back of my mind, I was insecure that no one else would ever propose to me again. The pressure of getting married had possessed me perhaps.

I looked and saw Saira. She was looking gorgeous in her simple baby pink ghagra—the same one that my mother-in-law had rejected for me. I looked at her with envy and said, 'I told you about that ghagra, right?'

'Yes, isn't it gorgeous? He also gave me a discount,' she said mockingly.

I teased her a little and then, under my breath, said, 'Looks gorgeous, you're beautiful!'

I wished I could change places with her.

'By the way, your makeup looks splendid,' Saira said, somewhat amused. She knew how much I hated makeup, and looking at my face, it looked like I had bought the whole of Sephora and painted my face with every colour available there. I felt like jumping off the balcony to strangle her for that.

I had changed since I'd met Karan. I didn't take things too seriously. I allowed myself to be mocked. I wasn't sure if that was a good or bad thing. But it just happened and I let it happen.

Saira giggled and laughed loudly. People walking on the street kept looking at us, wondering why we were talking from the balcony, or why we were dressed in a way that seemed to suggest that we were just a couple of characters from a soap opera. I couldn't help but laugh along with her at this. I looked at my outfit again and this time, I laughed louder than her. It's like we were competing with each other. I didn't remember the last time I had laughed like that. We posed a hilarious sight. If I were to look at two women like this, it would surely have made my day. Tears were rolling down my eyes. It felt like my stomach would explode but I couldn't stop laughing.

Saira and I walked out of our rooms together. The wedding processions had started. We stood next to each other. I was unable to believe that I was standing here for my own marriage. I had always imagined going to other people's weddings, but mine was unfathomable.

I wondered whether I was getting conned into this. 'Was Karan really the man I loved? He was the one I was attracted to, but love is a strong word. Did I love him?'

Saira shook me off and we walked. I wondered whether she felt the same thoughts as mine. It didn't look like it. She looked happy. I could feel her happiness from where I stood. She didn't seem like she was walking into a fire. I failed to understand that even though every cell of my brain had told me not to be married, I had said 'yes'. I never even showed any sign of disagreement. 'Was I being needy? Karan had shown signs of narcissistic behaviour in the past, but why had I overlooked it?' A part of me was screaming to stop this madness. But I continued walking towards the mandap, my legs moving mechanically. I was in a trance. I looked at Saira, and she saw the hint of terror on my face and she quickly grabbed by hand. Her hold calmed me down immediately. I took a deep breath and told myself—'I've got to do this!'

My mind calmly asked me the same question. 'Why?'

I was shaking.

Karan's mom jarred me. She could knock me down if she did anything further. Her excitement had no bounds. It was almost like she had never believed that her son would be married.

She was my amusement for the day, and probably for life. She was pleasant but laughed too much.

She walked towards me and said, 'You are the most gorgeous bride I have ever seen. God bless you, beta! Now you have a mother!' And at that, she stole my heart. It was heartwarming and touching to the extent that I cried and almost sobbed. I was amazed by my outburst. But she had touched something that had been buried in my heart like a stone. She had melted that stone. For all my hatred towards her for making me look like a walking jewellery shop, I forgave her. Saira too was touched by her kindness.

Throughout, Karan kept messaging me (almost every hour), saying how excited he was to start a new life with me. I felt like I was being unfair to him, but I couldn't get myself to send anything back.

When I walked into the wedding hall, I heard some people gasp. So many relatives I didn't know walked up to me to tell me that I looked like a dream. They warmed me. It felt good to be around people who loved you. Don't we all want that—people we love and who love us!

I could see Karan gasp as he looked at me from afar.

All our office colleagues were there to bless our union, including Mr Rebello. I glanced at him and my other colleagues and raised my hand. But my mother-in-law came up, huffing and puffing, to tell me that a bride should not act so casually.

I swallowed my urge to ask if a bride had to be uptight and uncomfortable all the time. After all, she was going to be my mom-in-law.

In dealing with my emotions, I hadn't seen the place. It was decorated tastefully and elegantly. It was likely that mom-in-law wasn't involved in decorating the wedding hall, considering how busy she had been decorating me.

Pink lilies were blooming around the periphery of the place. Jasmine florets formed a lace-like entrance on the mandap. Lord Ganesha's favourite, the hibiscus, was put in rows and rows to welcome me. The smell of jasmine mesmerised me and put me in a stupor. I was now feeling good about everything around me.

I saw Deva and Saira. Deva's eyes were full of love for Saira, and when I saw the same love in Karan's eyes, I felt lucky to be here with him. I was going to spend my life with him.

I looked at Karan and smiled, and he grinned from ear to ear. He looked funny and smaller to me today. I sat right next to him and he quickly held my hand when no one was seeing. His hands were warm and soothing. I needed his touch to get through this wedding.

The wedding ceremony was a blur. I did what the pandit told me to do—without knowing the reasons or even asking why they were needed. Throughout, Karan kept looking at me and kept talking to me. That kept me going. Of course, mom-in-law kept coming around to give me instructions. Everyone around was smiling; they seemed happy and joyous, if I may say so. I failed to understand why others were happy to attend someone else's wedding. Why do they beam with joy? Why is marriage such a big achievement in one's life? It's not rare. Every other person does it. Why would it make my neighbour happy?

I was reminded of Abhi. I recalled the unspeakable things we had done together while Karan was travelling last month. He was supposed to come to my wedding too. I wondered when he would show up. Abhi was good at detaching physical needs from emotional needs. And I was starting to master that act too.

But I promised myself. It would be the last time. After my marriage, I would try to be steadfast with the societal norms.

All through the wedding, Karan remained mesmerised by me. He couldn't take his eyes off me. He kept whispering into my ears, telling me how beautiful I looked and how lucky he was to have me. Every now and then, he cracked me up by telling me stories about his relatives. He was on cloud nine. At times, he couldn't contain his happiness when his relatives praised me; he took pride in it.

As soon as some relatives would wish us and turn around, he would tell stories about them.

'This uncle here bought a Mercedes to show off but he can't even afford a decent education for his daughter.'

'This aunt is dangerous. She loves to gossip.'

'This cousin sister has a secret side job as a waitress to support her dreams of being a dancer.'

'This cousin brother is useless, but has always lucked out. He got into the best college and now is walking into a dream job without working too hard. Lucky guy!'

'This cousin here is having an affair with his son's nanny.'

I giggled and laughed at every piece of information that he shared. It was nice to have a family, to call someone a mother-in-law, to have aunts, uncles and cousins. Karan had given me a life I never had. I owed it to him.

We were going to spend the night at a five-star hotel—as per tradition. It seemed a futile exercise for us, though it was traditional. It would give us some couple privacy, mother-in-law added. We were going to live by ourselves, so we would have the same privacy at home, but there was no explaining that to her. It was easier to give in to her request.

When I reached the hotel in that gaudy ghagra, I saw people staring at me. Of course, the henna and the wedding dress explained why they would, but I still smirked. Karan was holding me by my waist and kept kissing the nape of my neck.

When we reached the room and sat down, I realized how exhausted I was. We had decided to continue living in my apartment after the wedding. For the first time over the day, I felt like myself. Karan opened a bottle of wine he was saving for a few years. I had showered and changed into my pajamas, Karan grabbed me towards him and handed me the glass. We both cheered for us and drank in silence and peace. He stroked my wet hair and caressed my cheeks as if feeling the suppleness and the warmth of my skin. We sat close and he kissed me softly.

We watched some television and responded to the hundredth message on our phones, thanking friends and family who were wishing and blessing us. I felt overwhelmed and loved.

'I feel so lucky to have married my soul mate, Meera. Thank you for being my life partner,' said Karan. 'I promise to give you a roller-coaster life, with fun and love all the time. Whatever I can shower you with would be too little because you are very special and you deserve all the happiness in life. But I promise to give you all the love I have, and keep you close to me—like this, in my arms—all the time. Even when we have kids, I will love you the same, or maybe, I will love you even more.'

I was taken aback when Karan mentioned kids. It triggered me that he had thought about kids and I hadn't. But I didn't want this moment to end. This was truly the best moment of my life. I had found a place where I finally belonged.

And then Karan fell asleep, while sitting on the couch. At first, I thought he was only resting but soon, he started snoring.

I looked at his innocence and smiled. I emptied the bottle of wine and walked away and stared at the stars. I wondered where life was going to take me after today.

I looked back at Karan snoring and whispered softly into his ears. 'I'm ready for this roller-coaster ride, Mr Husband.'

14

The thunders and the rain raged. The weather was romantic. The cold wind blew and brought a splash of happiness to the leaves. The fluorescent green leaves and the fuchsia flowers beamed with joy as the rain fell on them.

This was my favourite part of the city. I liked walking around small lanes and seeing cute cafes. It was my day off and I had decided to spend it alone. I loved this freedom and I missed it now. I yearned to dance with the rains, bathe in the brilliant cerulean hues of the clouds on a clear and clean morning and wear the crimson sunrise all over my body. I longed to sway in the southern breeze with the greens. I missed the stage.

I stepped into a small quaint cafe and the aroma of dark brown coffee beans hit my head. I knew this was where I wanted to spend my morning. The fragrance of wet grass and mud created was the best companion I could have this morning. There was a nip in the air, which was ideal for feeling gratified and blissful. The tables and chairs were well-carved in an antique French design but were rather uncomfortable. The table had an iPad and service was procured through that. It was not my cup of tea, but I couldn't spot any waiters. Then it occurred to me that this place was self-service in its true sense. I had to order through the iPad and they would give me a name. And when that name showed up on the fancy display, written in cursive and golden, I would have to collect my coffee from the takeaway counter. The counter looked like a ticket counter from the seventies. It was a cool concept. It was different and I liked it. I had to get Karan here; he fancied these quirky things all the time.

While sitting and waiting for my coffee, I saw a girl in her early twenties sitting right next to my table. The girl was relaxed but her phone kept buzzing almost continuously. She didn't answer it. She calmly cancelled every call coming her way. She waited patiently for her name to show up and strolled towards the ticket counter to collect her drink. She sauntered back lazily; she didn't seem annoyed by the incessant calls. I was amazed by her calm and so I had to chat.

'Hi, I'm Meera,' I said. 'I just noticed how calm you are while your cell phone keeps buzzing. Normally, a person would show some signs of exasperation, but you showed no trace of any such emotion.'

She smiled back and said, 'Call me Naina, because that's what my parents call me.'

I paused for some time and asked again, 'What is your secret power?'

The girl blushed and her cheeks became pink. She was the girl next-door type; nothing extraordinary but she had the perfectly imperfect face. She was wearing a loose green short linen dress. She looked at each person that walked in. She glanced at them and continued looking, staring and not losing any eye contact. Everyone who passed by was annoyed by her intimidating stares but just looked away. I could see it; she was having fun at their expense—a small treasured joy. She giggled after every glance.

She moved her gaze towards me, looking dreamily and with a glimmer in her eyes. It's rare to find such a gleam and this young girl here had it.

So, I added again, 'I couldn't help notice you. Nice to meet you!'

I pulled out my hand for a handshake, and she quickly shook my hand. She had a childlike manner. She looked at me, blinking, innocent like a sheep.

'It's just work,' she said about the calls, discounting any importance given to them.

'Maybe you should take it,' I said.

'It's nothing, just that I threw a big one at my boss today,' she giggled like a teenager and then spoke again. 'I quit last night, over an email.' Her bright eyes grew wider and her smile gave away the ecstasy she felt about having quit. There is a difference between quitting and being terminated even though the final outcome is similar. The emotions that accompany them are strange. Here was this young girl, butterflies in her stomach over her achievement. Unlike other youngsters her age, she was not a conformist. I appreciated that.

I wrinkled my forehead as I wondered when was the last time I had met someone so happy about quitting. I looked back with a smirk and asked, 'So, where are you headed now?'

And she seemed to exude a calm at that question. She said, 'I don't know.'

Puzzled, my jaw hanging, I asked again, 'Why would you quit without something on your plate? Let me guess: marriage, further studies? What is it?' I kept speculating about the reasons for such a ghastly decision.

She strutted like a peacock and came to my table. Then, like an erstwhile buddy, she held her coffee with two hands, as though it would fall if not held in that precise fashion. And just like that we became buddies—in ten minutes!

I learned something. She was a 'sharer'; she dominated the conversation.

'I've got a problem at work,' she said. 'They have promoted me, and I don't want a promotion. Before I baffle you any further, let me complete my story. I work at a call centre for various online shopping websites, so my customers see me as a helpline. My job was to reply to a customer base who spent under five thousand rupees. There I received a lot of appreciation and felt good about helping when there were delays in returns or damaged goods or any such requests. Sometimes, I was asked to cater to the golden-card clients; the ones who spend more and were priority clients. But these clients never appreciated my work. They thanked me and were always kind, but I don't think I mattered to them much.'

She slid lower on her chair. Now she was resting like the rest of the herd, the forever slouching generation. I foresee chiropractors making fortunes in the next decades.

She said, 'Gratitude is important for me. These card

holders didn't make me feel good about doing my job right. Instead, they made me feel nothing. Now, I'm promoted and I can't work. I don't get the gratitude. But I have to look at golden-card holders!' She paused and then said, 'Plus, I like helping people who really need the help. The golden-card group isn't my priority, because they are mostly everyone's priority. I don't like to follow that path.'

'Well, that's a prejudiced outlook,' I said. 'They too might appreciate your help. Maybe you are being too judgmental.'

She raised her eyebrow and said, 'Maybe…but I don't want to waste my time and energy on what doesn't matter. I have enough savings. I will manage till I find another job. My rent is covered for six months so I've got time.'

This nonchalance bothered me and also made me jealous. 'Why didn't I take such rash, abrasive, unconventional, erratic, self-satisfying, self-escalating risks in life? I would never know life on the other side. The other side seemed far greener. What if…' It was quite surprising how this young girl had stirred these thoughts in me.

'So you just walked out because you don't believe in the job?' I asked, still flabbergasted. I thought I was missing out on something, but no, she was being candid. She was a refreshing and inspiring coffee partner!

I bid her goodbye after exchanging numbers and offering her an interview. She took it. 'She would be an asset,' I thought.

I immersed myself in the book that I was reading, but I kept thinking about this girl, intrigued.

Thoughts about the girl lingered even after she left, but

as luck would have it, she came back. She had forgotten her phone. I gave her an exasperated look and she giggled and left. This gave me the perfect window to ask her name again. 'It's Naina,' she said with a beautiful smile on her face.

I silently said to myself, 'It was amazing meeting you today, Naina.'

Her energy enthused me and made me feel powerful. I felt submissive in her presence. But she had cut across a secretive corner of my mind. It reminded me that I too had been frail once upon a time. My idea of myself was greater than the reality. I accentuated my emotions, and hence, I gave prominence to my views of myself. That was a long time ago, maybe a few decades ago. I now had an inferiority complex and lacked confidence.

My mind ceaselessly corrupted my understanding of myself till it was thrown right back at me. But my mind never gave up. It went on to convince me that I was right until I was proved wrong. I wasn't of the belief that I was always right, but egotistically, I did seem to have a superpower to evade the wrong and remember all the right, until someone I trusted rectified me. That was my superpower, my panacea to move forward. I dare not reveal my power to anyone, or else I might jinx it. I just swayed with the power. And when it eroded in me, I let it slip. Probably it made me a narcissist, but I really didn't care.

When I was in the sixth grade, there was a boy in my class. Most of the girls in school had a crush on him. Whenever I walked past him, he glanced at me like he was looking for something in me. I didn't quite understand what it was, that 'something' he was looking for. But I was blatantly optimistic. I thought he was looking at me. I made myself believe that he had a crush on me. It was unlikely but I was convinced. But I knew, if I talked about it, I'd jinx it. Keeping such appetising news from everyone had been hard for me, but I stayed on and he stole sidelong glances at me when I passed. A year passed and he never tried to talk to me. He just kept looking at me.

Then, when I was walking with my friends one day after our lunch break on the ground, I blurted out. 'He has a crush on me.'

The girls looked at me as if I was mad. They all secretly loved the guy and they were surprised. They thought I was probably out of my mind. At the same time, they had to snub me. One of them said, 'How did you guess it? Did he propose? Or is it just your wild assumption?'

I was caught on the wrong foot. I preferred to keep silent and just looked at her sternly. But that gave me some courage and I decided to speak to him, and ask him.

It was late in the afternoon, but too early in the evening. That time of the day when the sun, before leaving, empties colours into the sky and on all things. The earth, the lover of the sun, swathes herself in colours of life and in the warmth of love.

I spoke to him, and told him. He seemed to agree to all I said. He was impressed by my confident air, soft grace and also by the fact that I was different from those other girls. It was a conclusion that he probably drew from my attitude, or more specifically, my 'don't give a damn' attitude. I was drawn to him at first sight. He was too. He probably found love in my deep black eyes. I gazed at him, inviting him to dive in. And he did, unknowingly, unwittingly, but willingly.

He listened, mesmerised by whatever I told him, he was surprisingly in awe of me. I, on the other hand, was already in love with him and I made the other girls jealous. In hindsight, I should have thanked them for giving me courage unknowingly. But as all good things come to an end, so did this. They succeeded in bringing my affair to an end. Maybe I was to blame, because I myself was in denial.

I never knew what made us drift apart, but we did. After that, it felt like it never happened. I never noticed him looking at me after that. I never felt his presence. It was almost like he didn't exist.

It made me wonder if it was just a figment of my imagination.

There are many times when I feel like I imagine things, pushing the boundaries of reality. My inner world is so strong that I presume things. It makes me feel like I am ten steps ahead of the event. 'Was I creating a wonderland inside my mind?'

My mind was my protector and my guiding angel, but also my biggest enemy.

There were times when I felt dismal when I thought about myself. My idea of myself wasn't who I was, it was a shadow of others' ideas and opinions about me. No, there wouldn't be anyone in their right mind who would utter rude remarks or intentionally say something hurtful to me. Not even as kids. But I was intuitive—even when someone was being kind and generous, I could still sense their resentment towards me.

I tried to kill that superpower, but in turn, got blessed by multiplying it.

Then, I chose to listen to my mind, rather than the others, because all I heard others say was that I was dark skinned, that my armpits smelled and my hair was too thick. There were many of these comments, but my little mind kept wandering. 'Why then would men stalk me? Why then did they try to touch me inappropriately when we walked carelessly into the horizon? Why did they want to talk to us? Or do things to scar us? Why, if they were convinced about our rather unworthiness.'

Now I had grown older and seemed to understand the interests of men. The interest looked one way when they were in the midst of society and another when they were alone in the dark. They committed crimes at night and prayed in temples during the day.

After my coffee, I went home and wrote about how I saw myself again. I didn't recognize myself again today.

It was midnight and the phone rang. I personally hated calls at midnight. I moved in my sleep and tried to gather what was happening. Slowly, I realized that the phone was ringing. It must be family since my other calls were silenced. My dream—or rather, my nightmare where a well-trained and well-behaved dog was biting my feet—was shattered before it could shatter me.

Pulling myself up, I saw that my journal was open and a pen was kept on the antique carved wooden table. It was peculiar because I didn't *ever* leave my journal open, but that was something to scrutiny later. I was constantly interrupted by the thumping sound of the ringer as it sounded louder in the silent night. I switched on the night lamp and immediately felt stupid. The cell phone was flashing bright enough!

It was my mother-in-law.

Glancing over the clock, I was sure this wasn't good news. I thought of going back to my nightmare rather than picking up the phone. I didn't have a choice. Karan was looking at me with fiery eyes wondering who it was at such an unearthly hour.

I quickly gave the phone to him, showing him that it was his mom. Her photograph—a happy face in a bandhani red sari with red dot on her forehead and perfect teeth—flashed on the screen.

The happy photograph appeared creepy and daunting in the middle of the night. It was as if she was mocking us by calling at 2 a.m.

Karan took the phone from my hand.

'Hello?' he said.

15

My mother-in-law, or Maaji as I called her, and Karan called her Mummyji, was the one who had called us earlier. In the colloquial sense, Maaji is generally used in a specific context, i.e. when you give up on someone's bullshit in utter exasperation, while simultaneously promoting them at a level above you because they somehow manage to pull the brain out of your head and return it to you. That's someone whom you would call Maaji, and Karan's mother was undeniably someone who had earned this label.

Whatever nightmare I had that night, her call far surpassed it.

Karan had put the phone on speaker. He wanted my input in their round table conference in the middle of the night. After all, no one else was awake for any of her squabbles. We were always an easy target. In fact, her son was the easiest target as she was an ageing mother. The mother that never slept—my Maaji!

'Karan beta,' her voice quivered on the phone. 'Not feeling too well.'

I knew this was a continuation of the drama of the last month. She had pulled a similar stunt two months back as well, calling on the pretext of her health. She stayed with us for one month. This frantic phone call was a sham. It made me wonder why did she need these petty excuses to come to our house? We were more than welcoming. We had invited her a thousand times to live with us, but she had declined innumerable times. She said she didn't want to intrude on our privacy. And yet she was victim to these moments of weakness. She would lie to come and stay with us.

I would like to believe, and was rather convinced, that this too had something to do with Karan. He was cold and distant whenever his mother arrived. They had a difficult relationship; they barely smiled at each other. Of course, there was no lack of love, but there was a lack of warmth.

Karan looked at me, concerned, like any son should be. But she had never called in the middle of the night to say that she was unwell before.

Karan froze. He didn't know what to say and how. He held my hand. I could tell that he was nervous. He looked at me, as if begging me to talk and decide. I thought that was rather immature of him as Maaji sounded more than normal to me.

'Would you like us to come to you?' My reply was quick. I was seeking an immediate solution, just as the situation demanded.

Karan's grip was now harder. He was gripping my wrist and I saw that he didn't realize how tight his grasp was. He was worried so I tried to move my hand away. He made his grip tighter this time around, piercing his nails into my skin. My only way out was to complete the phone call so that his nervous energy would abate.

'Karan can come and take you to the hospital, Maaji,' I said.

To this statement Maaji quickly said, 'No beta, it's okay. You can come tomorrow.'

'No, Maaji, you aren't well!' I said.

'Beta, if you could come alone, it's okay. Don't tell Karan to come. It will spoil his sleep.'

I was amazed. Their relationship was something to write home about. She wasn't like a normal mother, bullying her adult son to the wall. Here it was the other way around.

I had felt suspicious in the beginning that Karan didn't live with his mother. Normal Indian family protocol calls for the family to live together, especially when the children aren't married. His scenario was different. She was the only family member alive. But whenever I had probed, he ignored it or snapped at me. When it came to family, we had an unsaid rule: do not dig deep, we might drown.

He dug into my skin, he was nervous. I was hurt and I instantly thought of chained animals in zoos. The pain was excruciating. I thought I would pass out from it.

I was angry at myself for letting him hurt me, but I let him continue, allowing him to do this to me over and over. There was always a valid reason, but yet again, the reason didn't justify the action. I saw that he was worried about his mother but I also saw a few drops of blood escaping my wrist, so I quickly took a call and told Maaji, 'I'm leaving now!'

While driving to pick up Maaji, I tried to analyse Karan's reasons for violence. He was a loving guy. I had noticed right from the beginning that his eating habits were monstrous. He was also conscious about not putting on extra kilos and did go to the gym. I found this tiresome, but it was none of my business to intervene and correct his eating habits or fix the way he snored. But I was seriously disturbed by his violence. I knew his problems were psychological. He must have something buried deep within, something that he is unable to share with anyone or find solutions to. He was not the type to sit and ponder on his own behavioural problems. He would go on committing the acts he was used to.

I saw blood trickling down the wound on my wrists. I had probably become psychotic.

No! I internalised my pains and injuries.

The next morning, I had an extra job. I had to feed my Maaji. Exasperated, I walked out of the room while Karan's drunken snoring drowned out the quiet of the house. I tried to ignore the recurring pain in my wrist and tried to make it go away. I threw a magic spell at it and it went away. However, I avoided thinking about it to not let the magic work. It drained my memory and the pain could not be found until something similar triggered it. I was a queen of pushing things under the rug.

Maaji was already up and praying. She saw my wound last night, and then again today. But she didn't say anything. She too pretended like it didn't exist.

I decided to put on a shirt. It was a hot humid day but I had to roll down the sleeves. I could hear Saira's voice ringing in my head: 'For what godforsaken reason have you worn a shirt in this heat?' I thought of excuses. She would believe an excuse. She wasn't naive, but she was in wonderland with Deva. They had a perfect marriage. I wondered whether she felt bad about missing out on details about my marriage, the way I was about hers. But she's better off missing out on the milestones of my marriage. We were supposed to be on a double date with them tonight; I wanted to run away, not too sure about the destination, but the plan was to pack a bag and see where the road would take me.

At the office, I was distracted by the shrill cry of the birds. The sound was penetrating deep into my ears, and it sounded like the squeal of a wounded animal calling upon me for help. The ear-splitting cries of the bird felt like cries meant only for my ears; I was the chosen one. I felt privileged to hear the yelp of the wounded, or sad, bird.

The sound increased slowly, becoming almost deafening, bursting my ears and settling into my soul. Everyone around me seemed oblivious to my struggle and the sound.

They were neck deep in the numbers that they crunched on their Excel sheets. They didn't hear the bird. I started doubting myself. 'Why were they not bothered by the screeches? Why were they indifferent to this cry for help? Why wasn't Saira looking up, showing concern. She had compassion!' After sometime, when no one noticed, I pulled my sleeve up to see the wound. I was starting to see it as a trophy of my resilience.

I felt like I was screaming and trying to be heard. Maybe I was the bird.

Saira, on the other hand, zoomed through the flashing numbers on the screen. Sometimes I wondered if anyone would understand. 'Will I always remain unheard and un-understood?'

Just because I had the strength to endure didn't mean I should endure. I knew this, but my ego let me believe otherwise.

Then again, this wasn't about my ego. I felt self-pity. I was defying myself to feel sorry about my state, and in turn, I was challenging my suffering to try and defeat me.

I now understood how women slowly become immune to cruelties done to them by their husbands. I, on the other hand, was not wanting to give up and kept trying to melt a stone-hearted human being.

There was nothing much happening at the office. Mr Rebello entrusted Deva and me with new projects every now and then and continued to bag the credit for himself. I maintained my dignity and kept him bossing around when there was no one in his cabin. I continued to give him unsolicited advice on his receding hairline and his guruji. Mr Rebello saw me as a necessary evil.

Deva, who had once tried to woo me, was busy in his work and with Saira. She was always by his side, and with her as a guiding spirit, he was sure to scale heights in his career. I wished them well in my mind.

My life was on autopilot: wake, work, eat, fuck and sleep. My mother-in-law was an addition to this life and a welcome change. She had aged a bit but was independent and friendly. She lightened up my mood every evening. She was a whiskey drinker and needed a glass of it every night before dinner. This came as a cultural shock to me that the same lady who had wrapped me in gold for my wedding and made me follow every ritual was not that uncool after all. She had her own idiosyncrasies, but fewer than mine and Karan's put together. I would say she was normal. In any case, every evening, she would pull out a glass, pour her whiskey and then add a little hot water to it and sit.

'Come, Meera, aja,' she would yell while flipping channels on the television to some soap drama. She had already set the table with masala roasted peanuts and wasabi popcorn. Alternatively, she would set up my bowl of nuts and an empty glass for me in case I changed my mind and decide to join her.

The agony I noticed on Karan's face while she was there was pitiful. At one point, his mother feared him, and at times, she would bombard me with facts that probably no son showed off his love for his mother like Karan did, and he was a mama's boy, etc. There were many odd things about them. But I stopped pondering over it. I thought too much about things over the last year and it had made me fragile and susceptible. I was trying hard to preserve my mental stability, because now, married to Karan, nothing made sense.

It was the same that night. While Maa drank her hot whiskey, Karan sat in the room.

'Aja, Meera, what are you doing? This episode will be over, and I will have to tell you the story again.' Maaji's high pitch got louder as the evening progressed, and I gave in and came over to sit with her. The one thing the mother and son had in common was that they both were relentless, almost to the point of being infuriating. Hurriedly, I went and sat down in front of the bowl of peanuts she had lovingly set out for me. The discrepancy was glaring. Now, after marriage, whenever we went out, I always saw a hint of irritation on Karan's face when I'd get a drink, but his mother lay out a spread every evening and I heard not a word from him. None of my business, but I was trying to understand my husband better. It might help me, I thought to myself.

'Maaji, can I ask you something?' I asked as an attempt to understand Karan better through his mother. 'Why didn't you want Karan to pick you up that night? Usually, people tell a girl not to drive out at night, but you chose me to pick you from your house?' I paused and then continued, 'It was an odd thing to do, wasn't it?' I avoided any eye contact with her after speaking, and turned my head towards the television. I didn't want to sound like I was questioning her; I wanted the conversation to be breezy. Maaji was far from intuitive, so I had to worry.

She too darted her gaze to the screen and replied, 'You know the reason, why are you asking me? Too often we lie to ourselves to undermine the truth that's inside us. We are afraid of accepting the reality. We don't want to see what's right here. Look around you, Meera, what do you see?'

I turned to look around the house. It was white, clean and neat, almost clinical. Why did the house shine? There was not a speck of dust to be found at the corners. The white curtains were pristine and clear and immaculate. Almost untouched. But somehow, they formed a strong barrier against the sunshine or the moonlight. There was one lone tissue box near the television and my clay turtles, which I had made in a pottery session, were missing. And my knick-knacks, which I had collected over the years, were all stuffed inside the drawers—no-man's property. There were no paintings and pictures on the walls, there was a perpetual echo or a vacuum in the space. It was rather eerie and emotionless. The temperature in the house was always freezing. I couldn't recall the last time I had opened the windows. It was the same house I had lived in before my marriage, but now suddenly I didn't recognize it. I got up and walked into the kitchen and everything was neatly kept. I wasn't untidy before, but this looked different. I didn't know I possessed such organising skills.

I looked back at Maaji with fear and trepidation in my eyes. Maaji was unmoved, still watching her soap. It was almost as if she knew what kind of black magic had been woven around me. I wasn't someone who believed in the supernatural, but it felt like my core was changing as I lived with Karan. And the hard part to swallow was that I hadn't even realised it. I was losing my individuality and my uniqueness. I was turning into the kind of person he wanted me to be. I was accepting all his nonsensical behaviour.

I looked at Maaji and blinked in disbelief, 'How did I not see this?' I continued, 'I'm turning into him, into what he wants to mould me into. I wanted to break free, but my eyes couldn't see anything that was chaining me to his behaviour. He hurts me! It is awful. It has felt gruesome and merciless! Still, I have accepted him and his behaviour meekly.'

I had been blinded voluntarily. I felt exposed and vulnerable. I looked back at my life and wondered whether he had forced me into making these changes, but he hadn't. On the contrary, I did it myself. I organised the kitchen to his liking. I let go of my colourful posters to make the house presentable for him. My cosy and reasonably clean house had been altered into white cold walls. I had turned into a neat freak. It's said that your house represents you. Was this my representation? Was I cold and distant like my house?

'Do I even feel like this is my house?' I asked myself. And the answers were yet to come, but I was processing everything at the speed of light.

'How did I miss this? Why didn't I see this?' I was not asking Maaji but wondering how this change had occurred without me knowing about it. 'How did I do this to my own house?' I wasn't an interior decorator, but my house radiated cheerfulness. Right now, there wasn't much difference between my house and a clinic.

Maaji replied, eyes still stuck to the screen. 'You didn't miss it, you refused to tell the truth to yourself. You wanted to believe something and convinced yourself that it was a life.' She paused and then continued after taking another sip from her glass, 'You know why I was so happy to see Karan being married to an independent woman like you?'

This time, she looked at me and said, 'Because I thought he would be different because you are different. This was why I kept coming uninvited to your house.'

'How did you know?' I asked, stupefied by the sequence of events unfolding in front of me.

She paused. She spoke with a tear in her eye, like a pearl that refused to fall. 'Because Karan is just like his father…'

'What do you mean? Like his father?' I asked.

'Do you know why I drink?' asked Maaji.

Anticipating the worst, I meekly responded with a shake of my head. That was my reply. I wanted to know from her about my husband, a man who was my long-standing boyfriend. I had misjudged myself as a scholar of human behaviour. I was just a person who had some facts and figures in front of her. I had never interpreted them. Looking back at my life, I wonder now how many slow signals or red flags I had missed. If I had caught them in time I could have changed my life for the better.

I was waiting for a miracle now.

It felt like an eternity had passed since Maaji had last spoken. Seconds felt like hours, despite the distraction provided by the regressive soaps on the television. It should have been an entertaining evening, with food and drink and conversation with one of my not so favourite person, Maaji.

But it was turning out to be a difficult night…

'I drink because I was forced to drink.' Maaji sighed and then continued. I knew that she was a drama queen and loved attention. However, I did not want to interrupt her. I kept quiet.

'When Anand, Karan's father, would come home, he expected me to first remove his shoes and neatly keep them in the shoe cabinet. I remember one instance so vividly, it is like it happened yesterday. One day, since I was in a hurry, I kept the shoes aside and rushed to shut the gas since the milk was boiling over. When Anand saw this, he calmly walked into the kitchen and stood right behind me. Karan was right there, reading a book. He was sitting on the couch with the cushions neatly tucked under his arm. Anand calmly stuck a burning hot rod on my waist—right above my navel. He spoke into my ear: "The shoes are dirty, keep them in the cabinet." And then he left the kitchen to take a shower. At that time, I wasn't sure if Karan saw what Anand did, but he never asked me how I got hurt.'

It was distressing to hear and my heart went out to her, but I still wondered about the drink. I can be insensitive when I don't see any correlation…rather, when I don't want to accept the truth. I strongly believe the human mind works in a way that we inflict as little pain as possible.

I leave it up to others to decide why I didn't react.

'Once, Anand returned home a little late and a little drunk. He asked me to drink with him. He knew that I was a Brahmin and I despised his drinking. When we got married, he didn't tell me about this habit of his. If he had, I wouldn't be his wife, rusting in his unsoiled clean apartment. He never saw the turmoil within me. It was like he saw through me and my emotions, like I never existed before him. He looked at me as a person who was his wife and was placed in his house to perform the duties of a virtuous wife. I, being a subject to his violence a few times, was now careful about his demands and his preferences. Drinking didn't seem a bad deal as opposed to being beaten till I bled. So that's when I had my first drink, which then became a weekly ritual. I decided to be a fish in the ocean since I didn't have a chance to be a mermaid. I swam into his filth like a seasoned fish, and then, life got better. His demands were always met and he got kinder.

'But I continued drinking. After a few years, it became my only solace. With Anand, when we had a drink together, we bonded.'

There was not a speck of remorse in Maaji's voice. She was a strong woman. I knew this now and respected her more. 'No. I hadn't respected her before this.'

But I wanted to get away from all this information. My head hurt.

What about Karan? I thought about how he behaved with me. I didn't want to think about those incidents when he had physically hurt me. But I wasn't doing a great job of it.

I downed a few vodka shots and tried to swallow my anger.

16

I stumbled upon some pictures of my life before Karan. I understood what I was really turning into now. I was dressing conservatively. I had a spark in me, which currently existed but seemed dimmer. I had a spunk that was missing now. However, it could be directly related to the boredom I was experiencing.

I got it; it had to be boredom that was hitting me.

As I cleaned the other cabinets, I also opened up boxes that Karan had brought when he moved in. I saw a few things I had never seen before. Looking back, I found that I hadn't changed, but my life had.

But looking objectively, Karan never told me to do or not do anything. I was always given a choice. I voluntarily chose what appealed to him. He was passively aggressive and also a master of manipulation that way.

Instantly, I was taken aback when I saw a picture of Karan with a girl. Likely his ex-girlfriend. I had heard from Karan that she was a gorgeous, vivacious, and progressive lady. I could see her glimmering in the picture and I wondered why they had split. I never got a real reason from Karan, but from the piecemeal information that he shared about her, all I collected was that she wouldn't conform to his norms.

He had once spoken about an incident when he thought his girlfriend didn't match his philosophies. They had a fight. He was upset with her about something and refused to talk to her. Surprisingly, he never mentioned anything about his past until we were married. I did not question him, since I hadn't told him about Abhi either. I believed that he would count it as a sin. He won't be able to register the physical needs of a woman of my age because he was younger and his sexual appetite was different. He would hardly have anything fair to say. But if I had known about his past relationship, I would have reconsidered my decision to marry him, or so I would like to believe.

But holding a grudge against him for this wasn't fair. I didn't ask, and so he didn't tell.

I recall the story he told me well. He said, 'She regained her senses during that one week when I didn't pick her phone. Sometimes it's important to make someone miss you.'

It had sounded fair to me. It *was* important to make someone miss you. I had asked, 'What was the fight about?' I asked carefully, without turning my head to make it seem like a passing thought.

He said, 'She had hidden something from me. She chose to not say.'

It took me days and weeks to think over what that could have been and whether she deserved to be punished for a week. 'Why does one have to say everything to someone? Of course, it wasn't cheating he was talking about. He would have broken her bones in that case. Then it must have been something trivial.' In the end, I concluded that I should let the thought go. It wasn't healthy for me to hold on to that kind of energy.

I still didn't know what it was and why they split up. I preferred unanswered questions rather than over-analysed presumptions.

I walked a few blocks. It started to drizzle. I noticed that everything around me was too slow. The air almost stood still. Perhaps the rains were necessary to continue this cycle of life. I dragged my feet, almost reluctantly. I wanted to be drenched in the rain.

It started raining, which was shortly followed by a thunderstorm. Mumbai rains can create havoc and they come mostly unannounced. But I love them. The rain brings out the spirit of the city. It awakens our sleeping souls.

The good part was that the road outside our apartment gates—generally busy with dusty vehicles—was deserted. Some younger kids were out playing on the road, not too far away from the smelly uncovered drains. There was no alternate open area in the vicinity, so they had adapted to it.

As I was walking slowly and watching the kids, I heard the noise of a vehicle behind me and I moved out of the way. The car passed by as it was supposed to and it stopped a little bit ahead of me. A man in a fawn-coloured shirt came out. He looked like someone I knew. Slightly chubby face and slicked-back hair. His tone was brusque.

It was Abhi!

Bumping into Abhi wasn't a coincidence. I knew his schedule. This was the time when he went to the neighbourhood coffee shop to unwind after a hard day of playing with colours and creating masterpieces. But I didn't want to know why he was in that car.

'Why is it that someone says this is a masterpiece and others say it isn't? How do you rate creativity on a scale? It is criminal to do that. Creativity cannot be rated. Something that pleases my eyes might not please your eyes or other senses. I might like the ocean while you might like mountains. So why is it that art is rated? Sure, popularity confers a rating—that's economics. But that has nothing to do with creativity. I call all creative thinkers masters of their world and their works masterpieces.'

We looked at each other and smiled. His eyes looked tired. I didn't want to talk to him in public so I moved away and ignored him. He got the signal and went in to have his coffee as quietly as he had come.

I went into the cafe. It was my happy place. The young college kids were hovering around carelessly, untouched by the grave realities of adulthood. I witnessed the innocence and curiosity in their walk. They were vibrating exuberance and vibing off with each other. Just pure youth at its best. Why do we lose our youth? Several studies have been conducted to find out what kills the curiosity that a kid is born with. When you are told the same thing again and again, it deadens you. It becomes a part of your nature. It had happened to me.

We aren't conditioned to look at the good side. I didn't see the good in Karan. I only looked at the bad.

I returned home. It was a ritual to sit with Maaji every day and have a glass of vodka as she had her whiskey. It relaxed my nerves. Saira, however, was of the idea that I was losing my marbles. But who was she to judge? She had Deva who made her life better, I had Maaji. She too made my life better. One's perception of better is relative.

So here I was.

I wanted to speak to Maaji about Karan again. I needed to understand Karan better to make my life better. Ironically, my life had seemed fine before Maaji had walked in with her big bottle of whiskey and her stories about Karan and his father. I was well aware that I had lived in denial, but never had the truth hurt so much.

Maaji was affectionate and caring with me, nothing like the maniac I had met on my wedding day. She kept trying to make everything look better, which was difficult but she carried on. She had her quirks and it brought sunshine in some way.

Recently, I got her some flowers. She exclaimed at the sight of them, and said that I was wasting money on useless things.

But all in all, she was a pleasant person to have around.

Karan's cynicism had dwindled; he seemed quieter when Maaji was around. I had always suspected this, but now it was confirmed. He felt snubbed with Maaji around. His little cruelties were kept in check around her. He had recently left for Delhi, leaving me to wonder what he was up to. He didn't send chat messages nor did he call much, never more than once. I was in no mood to call him either. We were not a lovey-dovey couple like Saira and Deva. They were inseparable. I got a peaceful feeling as I thought about them.

I know I had not been missing Karan, and I felt guilty. It had been a few days that he was on an official visit to Delhi. But my life was better without him around.

The motionlessness air was rather unusual that night. The air was quiet and the breeze was almost non-existent. There was a chill to the place and it enveloped the household in a vacuum. The weather channel hollered on about strong winds and warned everyone to stay alert. The weather department alerted us to a storm hitting the shores of the Arabian Sea.

I had been lying in bed reading when the clatter of the door handles alerted us to a menacing thunderstorm. The clouds were frenzied and grey. The gloomy winds warred. I got up and went to the balcony to salvage the day's laundry, which my mother-in-law had left. The winds grew vicious. I had to grapple against their pull on the clothes. I deposited the clothes on a chair and went back to the book I was reading. The plashing patter of steady rain was loud now.

It was a miracle how the weakest winds could turn into the strongest storms. The overgrown grass was still rooted to the ground, holding on to the soil as strongly as possible. It danced to the tunes of the wind.

The winds, one blow after the other, shattered glasses somewhere nearby and we heard the clattering. It whooshed like an unnatural ghost trying to take over. It roared about the atrocities of humankind. It was like we were being punished for the damage we had done and the filth we had left. The storms were here to take revenge against humanity.

The winds that once sang a lullaby to the birds were now harming them.

We thought that night would be our last night on earth. However, nothing bothered Maaji. She was unmoved by the thunder and the wind; all she did was close the balcony door. It was as if the sounds had gone quiet for her. Maaji poured a shot in the glass and placed ice cubes in her own glass. She placed thirty cashew nuts in a bowl. When I saw her so calm, my worries vanished. She didn't say it, but she taught me to live in the present.

Maaji was fun when she was drunk. She opened up and talked, more than usual. And I liked her nocturnal side. Give her a topic at night and she would go on and on. Maaji was more relaxed and she also cooked more. She hardly wanted to cook, but since Karan had left, she had been making her special dishes for me. On asking about it, she replied, 'He likes bland food, like his father. So one day, I stopped cooking and asked them to cook their own meals forever.'

'Rock star Maaji,' I thought.

'But you like chatpata food like me—spicy and mouth-watering, so I like cooking for you.'

I liked her character after she was two pegs down.

Since the storm had quietened down, the silence was inestimable. Maaji was mellowing. Her usual drunk hyperactivity was not to be seen. On most days she was like a teenager with an adrenaline rush. This was her age to be singing bhajans, but instead, here she was, with her whiskey glass. She kept offering me some, pushing me to drink like the alcohol was a magic potion of some kind. This was a peculiar change. After too many drinks, way more than what she was accustomed to, something in her shifted. Yes, normally people loosen up and it brings honesty to their communication. Some, like me, cry.

Instead, I was here, sitting with her in a dark room and not out with my friends. At that thought, my heart sank. I used to marvel at my friendship with Saira, but it had transformed.

Vodka helped me accept the crude reality about my relationship that I'd been running away from. We were at a crossroads. I cried at the thought and realized that the vodka was helping me cry.

After crying, I quietly sat at the dining table and ate the best meal. I couldn't recall a time when I had enjoyed a meal so much. My aunt often cooked a special dinner whenever her then current boyfriend would come over and this meal reminded me of her. She was a great cook, and so was Maaji. I saw a similarity in them. My aunt had a need for sex while Maaji needed her alcohol. I hate people who associate vices with a particular gender. Vices are vices—be it for a woman or man. But a vice can only be called a vice when it makes your life worse.

'This is the best meal I've eaten in a long time, Maaji,' I said. Tears rolled down my eyes. The emotions had been hidden inside and now they poured out, making me feel better.

'You are too soft to be living in this world,' Maaji said without looking up.

I hated being embarrassed like this, and that made me shed a few more tears. I wasn't weak though. I had just put my guard down with her and let go. When I started the day, I never thought I would sleep thinking I had no friends but Maaji.

Our time together was a time for stories. We both did what we liked best; she wanted to be heard and I liked to listen.

'Life can hit you at the most unexpected times, but when it hits you at an expected time and gives you no solutions, that's when we feel helpless. And my life with Karan's father was rocky,' Maaji said thoughtfully. 'I don't remember what led to what, but he was persistently harassing, whenever I delayed something. I had to do everything myself and at times, I would forget a few things or delay a few things in order to complete the other work. I was fatigued and burnt out, so my friends suggested that I needed to take a break. Carried away, I invited them over for tea. It was a wonderful day, and I felt ready to be by myself for the coming few months but promised to meet them again next week.'

She continued, 'The next day, somehow, Anand found out that I had friends over, so he arrived earlier than usual. And as soon as he entered the house, he closed the door and removed his belt and started hitting me. He wouldn't stop. I kept begging him to stop. I screamed for help. I yelled and cried. I tried hitting him back but he was stronger than me. He didn't answer my single question as to why he was hitting me but just kept hitting me with the belt. It felt like an unknown authority had commanded him to beat me to death. I wailed and bled; I was almost about to drop unconscious. All this happened while Karan was looking at me. He looked scared. I was worried for him, but I didn't know what to do. My mind was numb and my body was bleeding and black and blue on every side. I wanted Karan to go in the kitchen and close the door. I told him to do so and he did. I cried and shrieked as little as possible because I didn't want Karan to be devastated.'

She took a sip and I saw her eyes well up. 'After the nightmare was over, I opened the kitchen door to let Karan back in. He walked past me and told me, "Mom, you did this to yourself, why did you have friends over when you know you can't complete house chores on time."

'This was when I felt ashamed about the life I had created. I thought of him. He didn't think in the way I would want my son to. I felt more shame that night than pain. I then tried—for years and years—to change Karan's perspective. I thought I had achieved something quantitative, but I will leave it to you to judge.

'The key to making it work with Karan is diplomacy! You have to deal diplomatically with him,' she said and mumbled some more. Then she banged her head on the dinner table with a thud. She probably was exhausted after all the cooking and drinking. I quietly picked her up, held her by the underarm and she, like a quiet obedient kid, walked. She dragged her feet and finally slumped against the pillows on her bed.

That night, I called Saira. She picked the phone on the first ring. More than happiness I heard anxiety in her voice. She was worried I'd call her because it was an emergency, because I never called her this late. I let out my inhibitions and told her everything. I needed her desperately, more than ever. As always, she was cold and cut-throat when she told me the truth. Her honesty always made my day, but tonight I felt weak and shattered. We spoke all through the night. She told me that I had changed and didn't care about her anymore. Then, as though confessing, Saira said that she had started to think that she had lost her friend.

It was incredible, but I feared Karan's arrival; things would change when he came back. A part of me didn't want him to return. 'Was I ruthless to think that?' I just liked it without him. Maaji and I could endure together. I could see Abhi occasionally. It would be my little world, without any arbitration and any judgments.

'Wouldn't that be complete?'

Not having gotten much sleep, I opened the chat window on my phone, browsing through stories on Instagram. I thought, we are in an age where the phone is smart but humans aren't. In the new world, the technology we have made is smarter than us—they don't have emotions but they have emoticons. The human factor that they lack is emotion, and that makes them smarter. 'Will we also lose our emotions very soon? That's our future. We will become the robots we build.' It was such a low-spirited thought. I was not looking forward to becoming a robot, but I knew that one part of me was already a robot, and soon, in the generations to come, the other part would also be the same. This was to be our future when we become more productive at the cost of our feelings.

While scrolling, I bumped into my exchanges and banters with Abhi. Alright I'll admit it. It wasn't an accident. I voluntarily searched for his name and landed on his page. His artwork was displayed on the left corner of the chat window. He never put his face on display. He could have used a filter if he felt conscious. 'Doesn't he know that!' I thought, amused.

Fighting my will, I sent him a message, a tiny message. 'Hi.'

I did know what my helplessness was making me do, but I was vulnerable and I had had vodka. That's what alcohol does, it not only makes you defenseless, but also provides an excuse to be vulnerable. It allows you to take steps you wouldn't take if you didn't have anything to put the blame on. Alcohol is a perfect excuse!

Not expecting a reply this late, I continued scrolling. My phone pinged.

'Hi, you awake?'

My fingers were tired and I was out of my mind. The combination of tired and drunk is dangerous; that's the only time you do and say what you'd wished. We can be honest about our feelings and act on it without the fear around our neck.

At the first ring, I felt a cramp in my stomach, like someone was pulling my organs. I perched the glass of vodka on the ruined window sill and picked the phone.

In the stillness of the night, the ring felt like a fire crew rushing to an incident. The urgency. They were like hammers pounding through my head. I sprang up, quicker than a tigress, to pick it up.

As I said 'Hello' and heard him say it back, a quiet

calmness emanated through my veins. Like an electric current that radiated calmness rather than shock. My mind was tranquil and my heart felt sprightly.

This was the first time that I had conversed with him. It was like speaking to a different person. He was witty and had a spark that I hadn't seen before. He was aware I was drunk and he made sure to not let me say anything that might embarrass me the next day, nothing to make me feel like I've wronged. His conversation sparked off our bond and I understood that we had shared more than sex.

But I was heading towards disaster anyway.

He ended his call by making a statement: 'Not many find their soulmates, because they look for it in their spouse. But everyone deserves to find their soulmate.'

17

The next days were clammy, dank and steamy hot. Showers had been promised, however, as soon as it showered, it brought with it insufferable heat. It made the roads look brown and mucky, full with wallowing puddles. The deep potholes and the unbearable traffic made it worse. The sun struggled to peep through the persistent black clouds. The black clouds looked like a shield for the sun. It looked like a trooper for the sun.

My closeness to Maaji had brought us to a juncture where we had no inhibitions left. I was becoming a mirror image of her, more so to the sides invisible to me. It was evident to her. She saw that she blended into me more than anyone now.

I felt uncomfortable talking to Saira, but with Maaji, I was just repeating her history. Everything she had combated and withheld was being shared. It's safe to talk and share. I could badger and banter and weep and smile. Multiple emotions were accepted. The atrocities and the godlessness of the son were very similar to that of the husband.

Saira was blessed with Deva. She wouldn't understand the intensity of our lives. I was genuinely very happy for Saira and Deva, and took pride in being the harbinger of this joy. I felt responsible for her happiness as it was one of my prized achievements. On the other hand, it embarrassed me. It exposed me as someone who wasn't doing well. In this scenario, my ego crept in the form of excuses—I thought that she would not understand me, that she would discredit my feelings, that she could not relate, that she might assure me by saying that I was overreacting. The list was endless. But in reality, it was my ego. I felt inferior. I felt less loved and didn't want to emphasise that fact by lamenting about how I felt. She was my best friend, but I needed a mature ear. Bonds built over adversity are sometimes stronger than other bonds.

'What happens if I talk to him about how I feel, Maaji?' I asked.

The wind had stopped blowing. The tea in my hand had a thin film on top, a layer of thick milk. I hated the cream that accumulated. It was unnecessary and distracting, just like a crown.

The clouds were clinging to each other, warning of a thundering night. But the wind was suspicious. The wind wasn't accompanying the clouds in their plan of blathering on with a display of power. The wind had gone into some kind of a deep sleep. The dark clouds were lost without the wind, aimless and sad. It looked to me like a warning for sinister happenings. The birds chirped less and were tucked inside blankets of leaves, waiting for the lightning to invade. The birds were holding on to the trees as if it formed a shield in this battlefield of nature. A few lone birds were howling, probably looking for their loved ones.

'Does nature take revenge?' I asked her like a curious kid.

Maaji smirked and replied while walking towards the balcony. 'No,' she said, and then added, 'It just takes its course. You get what you give it. Nature is the best example of that. If you bite it, it will come back and take a larger chunk from you. Though that doesn't make it evil, it's just protecting its base.'

'Will you be okay without me?' Maaji suddenly asked. She was leaving, going back to her house; she didn't have any reason, no condition she could fake to stay on with me. She was now more of a partner than Karan was. I wanted to hold on to her more than my life. I knew I sounded needy, but I was transparent to her. My life was an open book at that moment and she knew my situation.

'Why can't you just stay here? With us?' I protested.

Having her around had been comforting. I felt safe in her presence. She brought calmness to the house. She brought with her a sense of calm that I used to feel before, which I once felt on my own. Now I had chaos in my head, my thoughts were loud and disturbing. She brought sanctity to my soul. She brought clarity. To top it all, she made me feel safer in my own house.

'I've been intending to ask this for some time, but didn't know if I'm trespassing the rules of decency, Maaji,' I said.

She just smiled.

I continued. 'When Karan's father hit you so brutally, did you feel like taking revenge?'

I knew the gravity of this question. I knew she would have to relive the moment and feel the emotions again. Her perfectly shaped eyebrows formed a V-shape, the sweat blobs on her temple glistened like waves in a tranquil ocean. The thoughts brought her closer to home. Her physical pain was distinguishable at present and I could see that the memory haunted her present. She had the option to retort and attack me, but she also possessed the maturity not to.

My eyes refused to meet hers. It was out of respect. I knew she would not like me to see her vulnerable. Even though she had shared many things with me, I had never initiated it. But this was different. This time around, I was asking because I wanted to know what was possibly in store for me. Historically, Karan aped some of the behaviours of his father—a narcissistic behaviour. But we were looking at a situation that had got out of hand. It was not in our imagination.

There was another part of me that had full faith in Karan and his love for me. The issue here wasn't lack of love. The issue was my self-esteem and the forthcoming annihilation of our marriage.

He surely loved me, but on his own terms.

The wind started to blow hard, abruptly and precipitously. It was a sudden storm. The flower vase on the windowsill shook. I rushed to close the balcony door, and I glanced over and saw Abhi. He was sitting peacefully in the strong wind, looking almost befuddled. He gave me a sidelong glance and a warm smile. His unswerving zest for stillness made me jealous of his loneliness. But my wish to always be on the other side made me wonder if I always wanted to run from my reality.

Soon, the rain stopped. The road glittered in the moonlight. Tiny streaks of blue sneaked through the grey clouds floating in the sky. The skyline on the west showed a hint of orange. Despite the clouds, the rain, the thunder and lightning, the moon came out of its hiding and spread a pale yellow light all around.

Maaji said, 'Yes, I have been brutally hit many times. He apologised to me. They were honest, authentic apologies and they felt real. I always forgave him.' She paused and a look of terror consumed her cavernous brown eyes. It was either bloodshot or tear-ridden, it was hard to read. The only thing that was obvious was the pain.

She continued. 'His skin colour changed when he was angry. He looked calmer than usual. He was disguised in a shadow. He was eerie. He was the storm waiting to catch me unaware. It felt as if he had a hidden calendar with the dates marked on it and that would tell him when to be a loving husband, and when to insult every living cell in my body. When the nightmare wouldn't end, I found solace in dreams of strangling him to death with a tight rope and enjoying his suffocation. Taking pleasure in his misery was my highest orgasm. The dream would end when I looked at myself in the mirror after his struggle, and saw a person I didn't recognise. He was in my skin. In reality, during weak moments, I could outwit my unhappiness. I was lucky, god needed him or god pitied my state and decided to call him earlier than his assigned time.'

'But still, who knows one's assigned time?' I interjected.

She continued. 'After his departure, I felt numb and emotionless. Then an almost unprocessed feeling of freedom came over me. I was like a mutilated victim, unaware of the course of action that she should take after her release. It seemed strange to be this way, untied and unchained, after being bound for so long. It's like when an animal is trapped in the hunter's nest for long enough to lose all hopes of release—not because they stop believing that they would be released one day, but because by that time they would have lost all hopes of living a gratifying life.'

'Do you know why I survived at that time?' she asked me and I shrugged.

'Karan. He turned into my guardian, as unexpected as that was. I needed the emotional security.'

The rain showered heavily on the palm trees. The dark green leaves of the palms were camouflaged in the eerie night. The tea and the vodka glasses stood on the windowsill and the crystals shone brightly in the moonlight.

'Our glass was half full, not half empty,' she said. 'Karan had turned our life from a living nightmare into a liveable suffering.'

The birds were drenched and unprotected as the leaves swayed away in the storm. Maaji and I sat at the balcony now, sipping on our drinks, not knowing when we would again share such a moment of peace and tranquillity together. I was happy to have found a true friend in her. She was no longer my mother-in-law, she was someone whom I could trust, with whom I could drop all inhibitions and embarrassment, and talk in a candid manner. She was the sunshine I didn't want to lose.

'Tomorrow Karan will come back. Stay. I see it in his eyes. He wants you more than you need him. Don't abandon us. We will sail through if you are here with us.'

I felt a lump in my throat. I had imagined she would say something else.

'The least I can say is that he likes you and wants you around. Maybe it's my inbred illusion that he prefers you around, and your resistance makes you feel unwanted. Many times, we don't see the truth because we are blinded by past experiences.'

I crossed my fingers, praying under my breath for her to live a little longer alongside me. I had the curiosity of a kid around her. I looked for her approval as she had turned into my saviour. I had to convince her to be my rock. Not only because I felt threatened by Karan, but also because I love Maaji. She brought warmth, assurance and conviction in times of adversity. The presence of a strong female energy was needed in this house. The thought of coming back to a warm motherly figure was welcoming.

Before she had come to stay with us, I didn't realise what I was missing. I felt like I did around my aunt when I was young. The similar smell of spices when you enter the house and food that smelled of home and mother's sweat. I wasn't ready to let her go. Plus, she was unrestrained in her way, like my aunt. I wanted her to stay. And I had made up my mind. I had to convince her. Mothers are easily manipulated. Emotional blackmail is the key to successfully convince them for anything under the sun.

And finally, the night of truth.

Karan was coming back. The return was as viscous as the night.

I had a knack for changing strategies so the wretchedness could stay on longer. I thought of the worst. I rarely worked with the obvious.

With my night lamp on its dimmest, I moved to the door. I heard the keys jingling as I struggled to go and open them in haste.

A thought crossed my mind: 'Open the door. Go.'

But my body froze.

I didn't know what had changed in the last few days, but I had built a wall so tall that I couldn't pass it either. My legs weighed unusually heavier. I returned to the bed.

At the door bell, I picked myself up. Seeing Karan standing there made me less nervous. My mind and heart said: *'He's the same person you fell in love with, what is bothering you?'*

And Karan stood there, staring at me, waiting for me to react to his return.

I made a joke in my head. 'What is he? Does he expect a trophy for returning?' I imagined him entering with a trophy in his hand and kissing it to show off. I used humour in times of adversity to keep my sanity intact.

He was standing there, flesh and blood, here once again. I looked at him and he smiled, a gentle loving smile. Any husband would expect his wife to spring up with enthusiasm and zest, but mine expected nothing. Today he wore the face of an angel. His scent filled the room and my senses.

I was drawn to him. I loved his intoxicating smell. I inhaled it like a drug, one I needed but couldn't handle.

I had to find a way to cope with him and his quirks.

He was not an angel but there were worse people on earth. I could handle a single devil, or someone who wore a devil's skin at times.

Despite the tension in the room, he dropped his inhibitions and walked hurriedly towards me—like it was an emergency. He looked like a mad lover who desperately wanted to touch, hold and kiss the love of his life. Like someone who had been deprived of something too precious for long enough. Finally, it was in front of him.

Now it was certain. He needed me as much as I needed him. Perhaps more.

Touch could make any sane person insane.

The comfort of a physical touch surpassed my fear and his anger. He was angry at the sight of Maaji's chappals. Because she was still here.

He grabbed me by my waist and pushed his tongue into my mouth. He chewed on my lower lip, lustfully and passionately. Not with any show of romance, he grabbed me by the waist and put his hands inside my blouse. This was when I melted and dived into the passion of the moment. I could even sleep with my enemy for this feeling.

He whispered, 'I don't know how I lived without your touch, your touch makes me want to live and try to be happy.' He moaned a little more and whispered with a swivelling sound. 'I need you, so much.'

I needed him too. I wanted him too. I wanted this to

work. I will make it work.

But I also knew that tomorrow I would be living through the same dilemmas.

In that moment, I wanted to forget the reality and embrace what was happening. He needed me too. My deep-rooted abandonment insecurities surfaced.

And I mustered all my courage and gave assurances to myself that I would make this happen.

I heard him moan, loud enough for Maaji to hear. Without feeling her judging eyes lurking on me, I left all my inhibitions behind. And while I was riding the pleasure horse, I imagined for a split second a distasteful shot of Abhi. I squeezed my eyes together, but it had felt unrelentingly satiating. That was a sign of moving towards disaster. It was intemperance and I accepted it. One of the deadly sins: accomplished!

Later, I lay there on bed, surfing through my dated Netflix choices and pondered why I had imagined Abhi.

I started going over the reasons in my head. '...Because you spoke to him last night and so he was on your mind. You wished it was him instead of Karan. The act was related to Abhi. Abhi was on your mind. Karan wasn't on your mind. You wanted to avoid thinking about Karan...'

Too many thoughts, and as they exploded in my brain, I fell into a deep sleep. It didn't want to wake up.

18

Maaji left our home after a few weeks. It's been some weeks since she left. She went away, taking with her my mundane mornings, my nervous evenings and my wakeful nights. I sat alone on the spotless white couch. It looked sad now, everything around the room looked sad. I needed some colour in my too-serious, too-prosaic life. She had asked me to slowly change the clinical white to some curative colour scheme. It seemed to work, especially in the evenings, when after a hard day of work and taking directions from Mr Rebello, I would settle on the chair very carefully. I would also, at times, fix myself a shot of vodka, very ceremoniously, and think about Maaji and pretend that she was still around. It certainly warmed my evenings. She was so full of spirit and love. She had sprayed my life with luminous colour and I was waiting for her to return.

I sat alone in the dark. My apartment looked like a haunted house in the dark. I was too tired to get up and switch on the light, then I realized that there was a massive power cut. The power cut had shrouded the whole area with a thick black film. The evening was uneventful, like any other evening and I missed Maaji again. She had left…

The winds howled at my loss. The sky wept with me.

I was alone with Karan. He was my knight in shining armour. He seemed to be on a mission to prove my worst opinions of him wrong. He did everything right. He never hurt me after that trip. I started believing that I might have been hallucinating in many situations. I was wrong. Sometimes, he said things about me—I was hand-wringing, and overthinking so much that I thought I was borderline insane. I was believing those things about myself. It made me feel that I didn't remember things or had suffered partial memory loss. Sometimes, I felt that I had emphasised on the enormity of the situation too much, perhaps a tad more than necessary.

He too told me that I made up imaginary or hypothetical scenarios, some of which had never happened. I was also made to believe that at times I blocked things out to make situations more pleasant.

But to me it felt like I was increasingly unable to do basic things.

Even at the café, the one I went to every morning, I felt alone and lonely. The need to chatter with people had lessened and lessened. This hadn't happened suddenly. It took a long time for me to believe that I was missing a link within me. Sometimes I don't know what I feel, or how I feel. I want someone to tell me how to feel. The burden on myself would be lesser. I sighed.

Even at an exquisite restaurant, like the one I had been to the other day, life still felt unsatisfactory, even while sipping on the finest wines.

I had been on a journey, a journey of life. I had heard the noise of the children and the silence of the teenagers. 'What changed these noisy children to become quiet lonely teenagers? Who is responsible for their noiselessness? Why do they feel the need to submerge their head, mind and soul in a cell phone? At what age did they stop playing in the playground, and when did they stop cuddling, and hugging? When did the kisses stop? When will they come back? Will they ever come back?'

The middle-aged couple with saggy skin were trying to hide behind the glitter. Their naked lips were ruined as they had eaten up the lipstick along with the noodles.

This was a place where no conversations happened. The mind was busy. The loud noises were inside. The outside seemed quiet and calm. People stole annoyed glances of their surroundings, at times with a grimace of pain, as they wondered how the world was happier, wealthier, classier and more wholesome than them.

The toddlers tried hard to jump out of their seats, but the distressed mothers stuck to their phones. The mothers were also training their children to be zombies.

And we wondered why teenagers were silent...

And here I was, sitting with Saira, my insecurities wrapped around me. I was being loud about how I was feeling.

Sometimes, accepting your weakness gives you strength. This was who I had become, strong but defenseless. I certainly was ineffectual, fragmented and shattered, but not hopeless. All I had to do was cut the extra skin growing on me. Sure, I was scratched and harmed, but I was relentless.

'So what do you think?' I asked after I had narrated everything to Saira. Everything, including details about my current mental health, my relation and indefatigable bond with Karan. I didn't add Maaji's stories as they would be too much for her. I didn't want to scare her off. I had to make her aware of the facts, and not give her reasons to worry. I also did not want to propel her in a manner that would drive her to jump to conclusions. And sharing Maaji's story would violate her trust in me. 'It's not my story to tell,' I persuaded myself.

Saira seemed agitated. She fought her anger, but it somehow came out on the waiter. She apologised to him later.

'I knew it all along. He is trouble,' she said. The skeleton was out of the closet.

'I had warned you. You knew I didn't approve of him. He was and will always be a narcissist,' Saira said. She spoke without looking at me directly. She fiddled with her glass of wine, fidgeted with the fork, continuously dabbed her clean hands with the ultra-smooth muslin napkin and spoke as if she were talking to someone else on another table. Her eyes were watery. I wasn't sure if she felt responsible for my state. Maybe she blamed herself for not stopping me from jumping into a raging fire.

Her edginess diluted the conversation.

But I didn't want to give up. It would be easy to leave it here. It would be awkward but it would end. But that would mean the end of honesty in our friendship. This would become a redundant relation, just like the other relationships in my life. It would be a friendship of convenience.

'I need your help,' I whispered to her, but it was enough for her. She had heard my loud cry for help.

'What do you want from me? What can I do to help you?' Saira said immediately.

'Please leave your inhibitions and assumptions aside,' I said. 'Now tell me what should I do?'

Saira was at a loss of words. She loved me too much to let me lose my courage. She had to be hopeful, especially when I was confused. But what she wasn't aware of was that I had been foolishly optimistic more often than I should have been. She was reinventing the wheel. In her innocence lay my distress. My life was waiting for an explosion.

'Give him another chance,' she said under her breath, almost ashamed of what she was suggesting.

Human beings are inadequate. They say something and mean something else. It takes one to be impassive and detached to say what they really mean.

Saira was screaming inside. She wanted to say: 'Leave him.'

But which friend would advise another friend to divorce solely on the basis of a gut feeling? Saira scrolled through every corner of her memory, combed it through repeatedly, but didn't find any reason to say 'yes'. Karan was deeply flawed and she knew it, yet she was reluctant to say that Meera should leave him.

In that moment, I had lost the most valuable thing I had then. I didn't have the old Saira anymore with me. 'She has left, she has left me.'

This verdict was served by Saira on a storm-swept, rain-bathed evening. The storm and the rain had claimed Saira it seemed, my closest friend whom I had known since forever. 'We have blown up storms over tea cups at the office, we have braved steamy heat and copious rain to get to the shopping mall... We have sworn at our respective bosses and dished out advice to each other about diplomatic handling of office politics...'

A slippery road lay ahead of me and Saira far away.

'So I just let it be? I shouldn't do anything?' I asked her.

Saira's rage against Karan disappeared at this moment of truth.

'Yes!' she replied.

'But you believe he is a narcissist, don't you?'

'Sure, but everyone should get a second chance.' She believed in what she just said. She wanted to give a second chance, but not to Karan. She wanted me to give my marriage a second chance. All she wanted was my happiness.

Leaves fell, streets grew crowded. People had come to this lane before. But this road looked like a dead end. This place was clandestine, private and sheltered, not to be shared with the maddening angst of Mumbaikars. Suddenly, my street had been discovered. It was exposed, the trees were naked and one could see through the branches. The once hidden haven was now open for everyone to see. And hence the haven disappeared, until next season. Just a few moments ago, it had nothingness.

The house was quiet except the sound of my breath in my ears. I moved around surreptitiously as to not make a noise loud enough to hear. Groping my way to my bedroom, I switched on the light. My gaunt face stared back at me in the mirror. In the dimly lit room, I felt as if the moon dust had suddenly dropped in. The crystal glasses with their shiny gleam seemed to look comfortingly at me through the mirror.

I turned around and saw Karan standing behind me. He startled me to the marrow.

But soon after, I felt a joy singing through all the pores of my body, playing on the strings in my heart an unparalleled rhapsody. I realised that the phone was ringing. I rushed to it, ignoring Karan.

It was her. It had to be her. Maaji.

∞

While walking on the street, I dwelled on my life. I saw my car parked in the corner, under the big tree. It wasn't a clean spot. It had collected dust and leaves had dried over it. It was becoming a permanent fixture there. The sight brought with it a memory of a moment when I had believed that driving wasn't safe for me.

It had happened suddenly and I wasn't to blame for the accident. The other car driver was partially drunk and maybe sleep deprived too. But I punished myself! If I'm being honest, Karan had instilled fear in me.

I was thinking of that day. It had been an out of body experience. Karan was sitting still; his jaw was clenched but he had a calm demeanour. He sat on the dining table chair and I was on the sofa. I was drenched and had a slight bruise on the elbow.

'I wasn't hurt at all, then why the drama?' I had asked.

Karan spoke, 'I thought you were in good control behind the wheel.'

His eyes pierced right through me. I just could not make out whether he was mocking me, or was simply annoyed with me.

'Yes, I do have control. He was drunk.' I defended my driving skills and was frightfully wondering why he had to take that guy's side.

'The passerby said it was your fault. You took a sharp turn.'

I was surprised. Karan had investigated after the accident, even before asking me how I was and if I was hurt. He had been more concerned about finding out how it happened and who was to be blamed.

'I took a sharp turn because he was coming right at me or else it would have been worse...' I had retorted in my defense. 'I saved us.'

Karan took a long pause and then said, 'I've been seeing you drive of late and you seem distracted.' He had a big brotherly note in his voice. And then, he took a longer pause. He sat next to me, rubbed my elbow with an antiseptic liquid and wiped my face with a warm wet towel. He took my hand and looked straight ahead, as though he was looking beyond in space, not focusing anywhere. He hugged me tight and then said, 'I love you. I will be scared all the time if you continue driving.' He said it with a finality in his voice. He didn't want me to drive.

He breathed slowly while talking, as though choking. But he meant every word he said. He wanted me to stop driving because he was scared. I thought that meant that he was concerned. He loved me and did not want to lose me.

It had all happened so fast and unexpectedly. I never imagined giving someone such power over my life that they could decide whether I should drive or not. Then again, I heard myself agreeing and singing along with him.

'I will take a break for some time and try to gather myself before I get back to driving.'

The thing about this is, we never gather ourselves. We never come back. We lag behind and stay there or go farther away. Never ahead.

Maaji tried to convince me to drive again. She told me I was cutting my own wings, but I didn't have any strength to fight anymore. I thought I would just flow. I will flow with the wind, I told myself, like a helpless leaf hoping to fall back on earth to regrow and flourish again. But that was not to be.

I was bound to be doomed. 'Doomed forever!'

Today too, like always, I had taken the car keys and kept them in my purse. Karan wasn't forcing me to do anything. I was doing everything voluntarily of my own free will. I was crushing my own will to grow into him. I believed I was improving because Karan thought so. On most nights, our discussions went towards what I should do to ensure my safety. The probability of something wrong happening to me was always high. And this was how slowly I struck off most things out of my routine. I even stopped going out in the rain. It was the worst thing to do apparently. I was in a golden cage Karan had built for me. And I let him.

It was hard to sleep nowadays, so I had resorted to taking medication. 'Nothing strong,' as my therapist said. I remember, I was the one who endorsed that I should explore my mental strength. But she, lady in a coat, told me things I once knew by myself.

I went to sleep early. It wasn't the effect of the medication; it was the effect of my fear. 'If this medication didn't work,' I thought, 'what will the coat lady make me try next? Am I an experiment, a guinea pig, for her?'

I recalled her saying, 'Let's try this medication and see if it works?'

'Is this a guessing game? Did she tell me to take these medications to ascertain how humans like me would react to it so she could use it on others?'

I had started to fear sleeping. My brain has associated sleep with achievement and I am an underachiever.

But I was petrified that I would not sleep.

So I forced myself to sleep.

'Maybe it is the medication! It worked,' I thought.

I saw a colossal borehole in my dreams. The murky borehole was covered with grubby green lianas. The well had steps all around it, vertical, oleaginous, algae-ridden rungs, all black in colour. Even a glance inside the borehole gave me chills. I instantly pushed myself away from the borehole. I was looking at the peaceful sunset and instantaneously, the heaviness left me.

I was floating in the air and the wind carried me everywhere. I moved to the bird's nests where they seemed to be preparing for dinner, and then I saw bees as they prepared for winter. The soft wind was similar to the sound of a mother calling her child inside during rain. A maternal presence was warning me tenderly, whispering words of wisdom in my ears.

Like every kite has its fate, my fate brought me back to the borehole, and it was right under me. My body was fluid, but as I looked at the borehole I kept freezing. I got heavier, denser and tighter. I hear the wind telling me to keep flowing, remain as elegant as the air, to not look down at the dungeon. The wind told me that the fear was in my head and it weighed me down.

But my eyes were fixed—I was looking for the bottom of the borehole. Alas, I could not find it! It seemed like an endless road to the netherworld.

I was still floating but was heavier now.

With my eyes focused on the borehole, I decided to take a dive.

And soon, I had entered the dungeon world. I was gasping for breath, trying hard to stay afloat, but fear was making me heavier. I was trapped in round dark walls. I glanced at the setting sun and suddenly I felt lighter. I was floating again. My mind told me to not look down, but my heart sank with the feeling. Even though I wasn't looking down, I was sinking, plummeting to the interiors.

The dungeon was deep and getting darker. There were ivies on the steps and snakes crawling through their way out in the light. I kept falling in. There was no end to it. But I was not scared.

I was just exploring, like a new world. The fear I felt

before was dissipating, and soon I heard a voice murmuring something.

'Wake up! Meera! Wake up!'

It was Karan. I had been speaking in my sleep.

'Is it a reaction to the medication?' I thought. The second voice in my head asked: 'Who are you trying to fool? It's your denial that has gotten you here. Stop it or you will die.'

Karan was vividly anxious about this event. Not worried, he was anxious. But I needed to not worry about Karan. I told him, 'It's the medication the lady gave me. I will just stop taking it. Nothing to worry about.'

I had to get a hold of myself. I was going insane. Inside I was shrieking, crying, yelling. I was telling myself that I was literally going mad.

19

As I walked into the dingy entrance of my therapist's clinic, the rain fell on my cheeks, tickling my senses. My triggered sensitivities had been seeking some compassion. I was on a quest. I wanted emotional compensation from a therapist. I walked into her cabin with the false hope that I would feel good about myself.

I wasn't chagrined about looking for help outside. Something was amiss about the way I was taking care of myself. I needed administrative counselling and controlling.

And I saw Abhi—flesh and blood. I pinched myself, wondering if it was an illusion.

Yes, it was him. Abhi.

Instinctively, I turned around and tried to avoid eye contact. After all, he was walking out of the therapist's clinic. These things were too personal. Not everyone was excited about spotting their friend at the door of a psychiatrist's clinic.

No, I wasn't ashamed. My days of being abashed and humiliated were long gone. When I agreed to stop driving willingly—to abate Karan's fear of losing my life over a trivial car accident—I had lost the will to live my life on my terms. 'I had let Karan overpower me. With the very thought that he would harm and brutalise me, I had given up. I didn't even try to protect myself. I just gave in to his command.'

My mind was full of thoughts, yet I kept wondering about Abhi. 'Will he actually mind if I call upon him here?' In the end, I chose to leave him alone. Turning around, I gasped at the iron door. It suddenly seemed like a prison door. My heart was thumping. I felt like I had just dropped my heart on the floor. I felt a chunk of stone stuck in my throat.

I peeped through the ajar door. I saw unaided and helpless people sitting on their ruffled smelly grey chairs. I wondered if I looked like that too, destitute and defenseless.

It was as if I was inviting them to eat me up. Piece by piece. My whole body.

I wanted to pull myself back to the exit and go to Abhi.

I needed a friend more than anything right now—a non-judgmental friend, someone who believed in me and my identity. I was facing an identity crisis. This could only be solved by someone who knew me, not by someone who was trying to know and understand me.

'I'm a complicated person,' I told myself. And I made up my mind that a therapist could not understand me like a friend can. These were excuses. I made them so I wouldn't have to do what's supposed to be done. So I did exactly as my mind told me to. I turned around!

It was a moment out of Bollywood.

I turned in a slow sluggish way, my hair flowing like dried leaves that were waiting to descend on the ground. My eyes glanced everywhere for Abhi. My shining armour. He wasn't in sight. I panicked.

I had finally, after many months, decided to do something that was contrary to what I had been told to do—see a therapist. My only chance to live was lost. I lost again to fate.

I scanned, surveyed, peered, examined and alas, panicked. My heart was racing at the thought of going back and slouching on that couch to talk to the woman who barely recognised me and also refused to comprehend me. She sat there with her predetermined and inflexible philosophies about me and my life, like I was a standard operating procedure. She read her prognosis about me without listening to me.

I walked away, faster than normal, and to my luck, Abhi was standing there, staring into his phone.

Without thinking, I walked to him. I felt rehabilitated, as though my lost powers had found their way back and were flowing with an unknown rigour in my veins. I could feel the rush of renewed faith in me, demanding me to swear that I never accept being crumpled again.

I was hopeful again.

'Abhi!'

I was loud.

He turned back. Then, recognising me he smiled the most affectionate smile. In my head it was a very melodramatic moment. But it might have just been a casual smile. My feelings, sensations, reactions were all haywire.

He walked to me and immediately said, 'You don't look great, is everything okay?'

There was no way to govern my senses after that. I embraced him and held on, for longer than a minute. I wished that I had married him instead. Just with one look, he knew I was hurting. He read my face like I alone could. I had never met anyone who could tell what I was feeling by looking at me. I felt loved. This man, who had seen me naked, understood me better than my whole universe. A tear rolled down as if accepting its place on my cheek. I hadn't felt desolation so dense and impenetrable until this moment. He then did the unimaginable. He kissed me on my forehead.

I was touched. I fell in love with him then and there. I was indebted forever, at least that is how I felt back then.

Later, sitting in his car reminded me of his dirty apartment. The car was distressed when compared to mine. I cleaned up. I assembled the books and magazines, heaped them up tidily, removed the take-away bags and walked to the garbage. Then I sat back in the car. He looked at me, smiling quizzically, like he could read the horror in my eyes.

'Tell me,' he said.

That was all it needed. Someone had to ask me and I would talk to a stranger.

I said it all. My thoughts, my feelings, my ideas, my fears, my paranoia, my illusions, my reality, my fate, my philosophies, my concepts, my luck, my doom, my strengths, my dangers, my worries, my thoughts, my experiences, my beliefs, my contemplation, my hopes, my wishes, my past, my present and my speculated future.

I needed this. I needed to talk, to tell someone who was willing to listen to me. Someone unbiased and not doubtful of me. Someone who would not disqualify my pains or judge my fears. I needed someone to listen.

After listening, he squeezed my hand, as though to fortify me. It was calming and heartwarming. It meant something to me and I was moved. I felt like an individual with an identity again. I had emotions. I felt alive.

He reached out and came closer to me. He surrounded me in his arms and I could feel the tears rolling down my cheek. I was overwhelmed. I wanted to hang on to him. That night, I slept without my sleeping pills, despite a sluggish monotonous sex session with Karan.

∞

Maaji was back, and so was sanity, or that is how I saw it at least. There was an understanding between us. It was probably loneliness that was acting as a common link, thus tying us together.

A couple of days later, guzzling my vodka and glowering at the golden-hour sunset with Maaji on my side, I spoke.

'In your absence I was made to believe that I was losing my sanity and was not lucid all the time. I gave up driving. I lost the confidence I had. I couldn't share my inner feelings with my best friend for the fear of being construed as spineless. I remained in fear always. I am sinking, Maaji, into a well, as deep as an ocean, in a place inside me that's lower than my reach, lower than where I can hear my own voice. All

I hear are echoes of Karan's words: "You need help with everything. But don't worry, I'm here. Trust me, I won't leave." These words haunt me. They have made all my fears real and transparent.

'I've lost my abilities. But that's not because I am weak. I was told to not do something and so I lost the ability. It's not my inability to do it, it's his inability to see me doing it. I've not failed. He ensured that I fail.'

'Was this his plan all along? Did he want me to fail so that I remain dependent on him, and act as he wishes?'

As I introspected further and spoke out loud, the realisation hit me fiercely. I was being browbeaten and subjugated.

On the other hand, Maaji saw the trepidation in my bloodshot and death-ridden eyes. She saw how I was being bullied. I was being conditioned to live the life of a slave. She wanted to hold me tight and save me from her own son. She wanted to cuddle me and wrap me in her sari and wrap me into happiness. She felt my pain, anger, derision and wretchedness. She too had experienced narcissistic abuse in her life. However, I understood that she could not fight my battle for me. She could only be my companion, and guide me.

That's when she told me. 'Leave him—or else he will destroy you. I was wrong when I thought that you could change him. He is digging your grave and I can't let that happen.' Then she smirked and said, 'At first, I didn't like you. But I now love you enough to save you. I was blinded by my love for my son.'

I was crying now.

'Go save yourself!' she finally said.

I did.

I packed the bags and was waiting for Karan to return home. I had to be strong, but I was scared. I was petrified. Suddenly, I realised how scared I was of him, of doing anything against him. To an outsider this might seem petty, but the mental distress I felt each time I saw him was even worse than any physical pain. It felt like every part of my body was aching in pain in his presence. It was natural for nervousness to creep in.

He walked into the house and saw that there was a big suitcase that seemed fully packed. He immediately understood that I had packed all his belongings into this suitcase. Knowing me, he knew that this was the end. Packing that baggage inside of me was step one, packing up his belongings only resonated my firm decision. I had turned back into my old self. Ignoring the reality, he walked past me.

'What's for dinner?' he said.

'Aloo paratha,' I said.

After dinner, seated on the table right opposite him, I felt calm and unruffled. This was the moment my fear died. I felt power I had not known within me. I could stand up and live an honourable life. After eating, I handed the bags to him and asked him to leave.

I was ready with ammunition if he revolted. But he went silently.

That night, and the next day too, I slept. I slept peacefully. I was not sure what to do next. So I just slept through the day, and night.

I called Saira after that and I cried. Like a true friend, she came over with wine and ice cream. I felt good.

'It was over. The nightmare was finally over!' I could feel a sense of relief wash over me. And since then, life has been good and uneventful again.

20

Life is good again. I have been free from that narcissist for two years now. I have joined my office again and have been working quite seriously. Surprisingly, Karan had left his job, maybe embarrassed that I left him. I have started driving too. I have regained some confidence in myself. But I don't have the appetite to get into a relationship. Abhi remains a dear friend.

On Sunday morning, Saira and I were at a mela, not too far from my house. The plan was to stroll around a little, eat some goodies and be back home by lunch.

While walking towards the cotton candy stall, I saw Karan.

I froze. This was the first time that I was seeing him after the divorce. My hands and legs went numb. Saira saw me and immediately diverted my direction and pulled me backwards.

Then, I heard someone calling out Karan's name. It was a woman. I wanted to run up to her and tell her not to marry him or be around him. My natural instinct was to save her from him, to keep her away from this narcissistic ex-husband of mine. He was an abuser and she would be violated, I knew it.

As I took a step towards her, I saw something I didn't expect. There was a kid with her. My eyes were blurry with tears and my head was spinning. I couldn't believe what I was seeing. The kid seemed around ten years old.

Saira was as dumbfounded as me. For a moment, I didn't know what was happening. I didn't believe it.

The kid walked up to Karan. He said, 'Dad, can I buy that?'

He was Karan's son. 'How is this possible? Karan was married to me... How could he be married to someone else too?' My head was spinning.

Right there, tears started rolling down my eyes. I again felt like a broken person. I had no idea how long I would take to heal from this new wound.

Moments take time to die. They take days. Sometimes they are present in every breath. Memories live on. They appear with distant sounds, a touch or a smell. They return when you see a face too. But you continue to live on! Because, after all, nightmares too come to an end.

No one knows when the nightmares would end, but when they do end it won't matter much. When the wound is healed, and the wound doesn't seem like a wound but a learning, that is when the nightmares end. Then, they don't haunt you, but just make you stronger and inspire you to help other victims who can't find the light.

So, it is the survivors who have to overcome through strength, and spread the light of resilience and hope.